THE BOY

ALAN SAKELL

Fulton Books, Inc.
Meadville, PA

Published by Fulton Books 2021

ISBN 978-1-64952-839-1 (paperback)
ISBN 978-1-64952-841-4 (hardcover)
ISBN 978-1-64952-840-7 (digital)

Printed in the United States of America

To the two most important women in my life:

Bryttany, the best daughter a father could ever hope for.

Doris, the best mother a man could ever ask for.

I love you both so much!

THE SESSIONS

1

DR. FRANK

I have a new patient coming in tomorrow morning whom I have been looking forward to meeting for quite some time now. I, like pretty much every other person with any kind of curious mind, have been following his story since it all began years ago. I couldn't believe it when I received word that I would be the lucky one who would get to work with him. Although I already knew most of the story, I printed out every article I could find online to make sure I was as ready for his arrival as I could be. I have never been so anxious to sit across from a patient as I am now. I have been counting down the days for weeks, and it is finally happening tomorrow.

I have so many questions I want to ask him that I am not even sure where I should begin. I hope he is ready for this. I do not want to have to force him to open up to me. I want him to feel like he can tell me anything and everything that he can remember going back as far as he can. I need him to know that he can trust me, which from what I know already is going to be very hard for him to do. After what he has been through, I am sure trust will not come easily. I will have to start earning his trust from the very first minute we meet.

I plan on spending the remainder of the day rereading as many of the articles I found as I possibly can. I want to have every detail that has been printed about him fresh in my mind. I do not like meeting new patients without knowing as much about them as I can before they show up at my office. I have had quite a few patients that come to see me and immediately start lying about every little thing they can. It is usually out of fear, I believe. They are not used to having someone they can trust with their innermost secrets. I always have to break down the barriers they have had in place for years, which can take a very long time to do.

The more I know upfront, the less time I need to spend weeding through the lies. I try to not just call them out on their lies but also question what I know to not be the truth, sooner rather than later. I think it helps them to trust me when they realize I have actually spent time trying to get to know them as much as possible before our first session. I always treat them the way I would want to be treated, honesty and mutual respect go a long way. This will be the beginning of what could be a very long road. One mistake that a lot of other therapists continue to make is they try to hurry things along too quickly. They are in such a rush for a favorable outcome that they can actually cause a very negative experience for their patients, which can in turn get them a less than accurate result. One day at a time is the only way this process works. Building trust is the key to the success of any kind of relationship, and trust cannot be forced or rushed; it needs to be earned.

I cannot help but wonder if he is as anxious to meet me as I am to meet him. I know through the years a few other therapists have tried to get through to him, but none have been successful. I am very good at my job. I take it very seriously no matter who my patient is. I chose this profession because I want to help people that need me. It is a very rewarding job when done properly. I have no intention of failing. I will not let him down.

I take all my printouts of the articles, which fills quite a few folders, and cozy up on my sofa for a long night of reading. I shut the ringer off on my cell phone so I can stay as focused as I possibly can. Tomorrow is the big day, the day I meet the boy, the boy who became the man whom everyone wants to know all about.

CHAPTER
2

THE BOY

They bring me to my new therapist's office at 9:00 a.m. on the dot. I am impressed immediately by the decor he has selected. It gives his office a homier feel than the last few I have been in. Dr. Frank looks a lot younger than I expected him to. He cannot be much older than I am. He is either aging well, or he is a recent graduate. He greets me at the door and offers me his hand to shake, which also impresses me. He has a friendly smile and kind eyes. There is some sort of mellow music playing very lowly, which I assume is meant to have a calming effect, but for some reason, I find it very distracting. My mind tends to wander quite often, and I can already feel it starting to follow along with the music and blocking out Dr. Frank. He seems to notice I am drifting almost as quickly as I do and walks over to the sound system and shuts it off. He is very perceptive, which will come in handy the more time we spend together.

He asks me if I would like to sit down and points to the chairs near the window. I wait for him to sit down first to make sure I sit in the chair that is meant for me, but he does not move at all. I think he is waiting to see which chair I will pick. Is he testing me already or just being polite? Instead of sitting, I walk over to the windows and check out the view. It has been quite a long time since I have seen a view this nice. We are on the fifth floor, and there are no taller buildings around us to block my view, so I can see pretty far in the distance.

Dr. Frank walks up beside me and joins me at the window, he asks me the first of many questions he will ask me over time, and I answer him with the first thing that pops into my mind, which is a very bad habit of mine. He asks, "What do you see when you look out there?" to which I reply, *"Freedom."* I have not felt free for as long as I can remember. For one reason or another, my life has not been my own since I was very young, and I honestly do not think I will ever feel free again.

I half expect him to push me for more on the subject, but instead he just extends his arm, points over to the chairs, and simply says, "Shall we?" This time I do not wait for him to sit down first. I had actually picked out my chair the second I walked into his office. When you live the life I have lived, you try your best to never have your back to a door. You always want to be facing it so no one can sneak up on you when you least expect it. With that in mind, I walk over to the chair that allows me to see the door and sit down. Before he joins me, he offers me a drink of water, which I accept. He fills two glasses with water and a few ice cubes, hands one of them to me, then he takes his seat facing me. He is only about six feet away from me, which would normally make me uncomfortable, but there is a sort of calming, reassuring feeling about him. I can tell he wants me to feel relaxed with him; he is letting me lead the way so far. I like your style, Dr. Frank.

Once we are both settled into our chairs and have both drank some of our water, he grabs a notebook and a pen from the table that is between us, and he starts writing. I cannot imagine what he is writing already because he has not even started trying to analyze me yet. Out of curiosity, I ask him what it is he just wrote in his notebook; he picks it up off his lap and turns it around so I can read it. In big letters across the top of the page, in all capital letters, is the word "FREEDOM." I think Dr. Frank and I are going to get along just fine.

CHAPTER
3

DR. FRANK

Freedom, I have looked out the windows in my office hundreds of times and never once had I seen freedom. From the second I heard him say it, I knew he was ready. I also realized in that same second that the word "freedom," to him, had more than one meaning. He of course wants the freedom that we all take for granted these days: the freedom to make our own choices, allowing us to do what we want to do, how we want to do it, and when we want to do it.

But as I sit across from him now, I can see very clearly that the freedom that is most important to him is the freedom from himself. I may not have the power to give him the freedom to make his own choices, but I am going to do all I can to give him the freedom from himself.

Although I know from the articles I have read that he is now a twenty-eight-year-old man, I also know that if I have any chance of helping him, I need to start our sessions as if I am talking to the nine-year-old boy he once was and, in some ways, still is. I am hoping that he will trust me enough to go back even further in time. I want to go back as far as his memory will allow us to go. To get the complete story, we will need to start at the very beginning, no matter how painful it may be for him. One day at a time for as long as it takes.

I must admit, hearing his response of "Freedom" has thrown me off a bit. I had a complete list of questions ready to go for our first session today, but now I am not sure if I should change it up a bit. Should I ask him to elaborate on his response, or should I just let it linger there like a ghost neither of us want to admit we can see? He meets my eyes for the first time, and I feel an instant connection with him. It is so clear to see that he is incredibly sad, lonely, terrified, and completely lost. He needs me, and I need him to know he can trust me and count on me no matter what he has or has not done.

It is like he can read my mind; he knows I am struggling with where to start, and it is making him uncomfortable, which is causing him to start drifting off again, which neither of us want. I have found that most of my patients are more comfortable and trusting when we refer to each other by our first names. It can be stressful and/or intimidating for them to always be calling me doctor, which is very understandable, even though I have been younger than quite a few of them. I am not sure what he wants me to call him. I certainly do not want to call him "the boy." I am pretty sure he is the first patient I have worked with who has asked me a question so soon: "I was wondering if it would be okay with you if I called you Dr. Frank?" Interesting, as I am sitting here contemplating which question to ask first while also trying to figure out how he would be most comfortable with me addressing him, he asks me that question. Which one of us is the doctor, and which one of us is the patient?

"You can absolutely call me Dr. Frank if you like," I respond, which I immediately follow up with, "What shall I call you?" leaving the decision to him. This is the question I have pondered more than any other since the day I found out I was going to be working with him. Because he was only nine years old when the story made front page news, they held back his name; he became known as "the boy." In every single article I read yesterday, for probably the tenth time, he is always referred to as the boy.

I am pretty sure I have seen or heard his birth name once or twice, but I do not know how he would react if I called him by it or if it is even his real name. I could have searched his file they have on him or dug into birth records, but again, this is about the trust we build between us. I do not want him to question any of my actions.

CHAPTER

4

THE BOY

Very well played, Dr. Frank! He may be young, but he sure knows what he is doing. I may have finally met my match. All the rest of the doctors they have stuck me with through the years had absolutely no clue what they were doing. They did not understand what I needed from them to make me want to give them what they so badly wanted from me. It has been almost twenty years that I have been living my life of hell with not even the slightest bit of hope for any kind of freedom, but right now, at this very moment, as I look at Dr. Frank, I can't help but wonder if he wants it for me too.

"That depends, Dr. Frank," I respond back to him. After all that I have been through in my life, he must realize that I am not going to just trust him instantaneously. There have been only two people whom I have ever truly trusted in my life, and they both just vanished on me one day. They knew how much I needed them, but they obviously did not feel the same way. I have never recovered from that. I swore that day I would never make that mistake again.

He looks at me with a bit of a confused look on his face, which surprises me a little. I know he specializes in unreachable patients like me, so my response should have been at least remotely expected. He reaches over, picks up his glass of water, and takes a small sip, just enough to wet his lips and fill the awkward void of silence between us. He is being overly cautious with me, which is making me want to open up to him if even just a little bit for now.

He puts his glass back on the table and tries again. "At this very moment, while you are sitting here in this office with me, if you could change your name to any name at all, what would it be?" Okay, Dr. Frank, I see where you are going with this. You are taking a very different approach than all the other doctors have tried, and I have to say I am indeed very impressed again by you. I cannot remember the last time anyone has made me feel like I was the important one in the room. In all honesty, this may be the first time ever in my life.

Now my mouth is feeling dry. I take a sip of my water, notice the ice has already completely melted, and put the glass back down, making sure it lands right over the ring of water that has been left behind on the table. I again meet his eyes and tell him my answer, "Bryant, with a *Y*," I say. I have always liked that name more than my real one. I don't think I have ever heard it as a person's name before, though I have as the name of a school or college. He looks at me with just one eyebrow raised a bit and says, "Bryant with a *Y* it is."

We have only been in Dr. Frank's office for a short time, and I am already feeling exhausted. I have been on so many different medications throughout the years, always feeling like I have been living in a fog, but Dr. Frank was very persistent that they stop all my medications for a complete month before our sessions started. This last month has been like being stuck on an emotional roller coaster that I could not find the exit for, which has left me feeling tired for most parts of the days. It has also made my mind start to wander more often, which I do not like. It brings me back to my childhood, and that is not a place any sane person would want to revisit, though I suspect that is the exact reason Dr. Frank was so persistent. I sure hope he does not regret that decision.

I notice he has started writing in his notebook again. I am assuming he is writing down the name Bryant so he won't forget it when we have our next session. Hopefully I will not forget it either or choose a different one. If he thinks I am going to make this easy for him and just spill my guts, he has me seriously mistaken with someone else. That will never happen. If you want to know, Dr. Frank, you are going to have to ask me.

5

DR. FRANK

Now that we are on first-name basis, it is time for me to start testing the waters. I need to find out where he is at emotionally since he has been off his medications for a month. I can tell just by looking at him that he is a bit drained physically, which is to be expected, but it is his emotional state, that I am more concerned with. If the medications have not fully made it out of his system, he may still be difficult to reach. I do not want to waste my time or his time.

And so it begins, "Bryant, I am assuming you know why you are here meeting with me this morning?" to which he simply nods his head. That is not the reaction I was hoping for. I want him to use his words with me. In my experience, it is always good practice to give as little information as possible. It is better to let the patient tell you their story rather than you trying to tell it for them. Maybe he is not as ready as I thought he was.

"I want to help you deal with what you have lived through in a safe space. I want you to be able to trust me and feel comfortable telling me anything that you can remember, that will help me get you the freedom you want. Does that sound like something you would be interested in trying with me?" It is very important for me to keep in mind everything that I already know about him, or at least everything that I have read, which may or may not be 100 percent accurate. I need to pay attention to the words that I choose when I speak to him. I have had a few patients in the past who have lived through very similar circumstances, though not as extreme, and they all seemed to have trigger words that would instantly put them back in the midst of their trauma and would cause setbacks in our progress every time. The problem is that I do not know what the trigger words may be until I actually use them.

I have already caught onto something interesting about him: he only makes eye contact with me when he is going to speak. I am not sure what is causing that. It could just be shyness or that he is not comfortable being around me, especially with me this close to him. Then, just as expected, he looks me in the face and says, "I would like to give it a try, Dr. Frank." He is not saying much, but at least he is saying something. Some patients will not even say a word until we have had at least three sessions together. It is extremely difficult to learn anything about a patient when they will not partake in the sessions. They will just sit there and look at me like I am an alien from another planet.

I have a feeling I am going to get much more out of him if I let him think he is running the show. I can see it in his eyes when he actually looks at me, that he wants to talk to me, that he wants me to help him. I have looked into enough blank stares to know when I am dealing with a lost cause, and that is not what I am seeing in his eyes. I will definitely not mention this to him or write it down in my notes, but he has incredible blue eyes.

"That is really great to hear, Bryant. I am wondering if there is anything in particular you would like to talk to me about today. Something from your childhood perhaps? A good memory or a bad memory, anything at all that comes to mind. There is absolutely nothing that you cannot talk to me about. Think of me as your own private confidant." Another thing I have already picked up on is that I absolutely cannot read his face. He could either be thinking that he wants to talk to me until he is out of breath or that he wants to jump right out those windows looking for freedom. His face is giving nothing away.

Without saying a word, he stands up, picks up his glass from the table, walks over to the other table with the pitcher of water on it, drops a few ice cubes in his glass from the ice bucket (which is most likely more water than ice by now), then fills his glass the rest of the way with water from the pitcher. He then walks back to his chair, sits down, and takes a drink from his glass before placing it back on the table in the same exact spot it was before. Once he is comfortably situated in his chair across from me again, he looks at me; with the most serious tone in his voice, he says, "I did not kill my parents."

I pride myself on being very professional inside and outside of my office, but I may need a backhoe to come lift my jaw back into place after what he just said. He caught me completely off guard, which is not easy to do. I am usually prepared for anything my patients may say to me, but for him to just blurt out "I did not kill my parents" during our first session was something I had not expected. He knows he got to me with that one as I just sit here and look at him like a deer in very bright headlights.

I do not want to push him too hard, especially during our first session, but can I really just let the subject drop? His eyes instantly lost contact with mine after saying it, which tells me he does not plan on following his statement up with anything else. He is waiting to see what I will do. The next thing I say or ask him may end up being very pivotal in the outcome of our sessions. I am trying so hard to read him, but it is not working at all. I have no idea if he proclaimed his innocence to me so soon in hopes of me following up on it with him or in hopes of me just letting it go and moving on. Every patient is different, especially the hard-to-reach ones. Being able to read them, no matter how little, is always a humongous help. He is not making this easy for me at all.

I am going to follow my instincts. I am pretty certain he wants to talk to me. He wants to get the past off his chest; he wants me to help him find his long-lost freedom. I cannot, will not fail him like everyone else has in his life. I will proceed with caution, at least for today's session, but I will proceed nonetheless.

"Is that something you would like to get more into today, or would you like to start with something else?" I am hoping that by leaving the decision to talk further about his parents' deaths up to him, he will see I am one of the good guys. I am on his side, even if he is not one of the good guys. If I push too hard and force him to talk about it before he is ready to, he may feel like I have put him in a corner, which may cause him to shut down on me. That is the last thing I want to do.

He shimmies a bit in his chair as if his ass has fallen asleep on him. These are not the most comfortable chairs to spend a long time sitting in, but that is on purpose. Studies show that if a patient gets too comfortable, they may take longer to open up because they would be allowed more sessions, thus more time in a comfortable chair. I am not totally convinced I believe that theory, which is why I have replaced the chairs twice already. It is not just the patients that are sitting for an hour at a time in an uncomfortable chair. I am practically on the edge of my seat waiting for his response as it is.

To my relief his eyes move to mine. My anticipation of his next words is making me wish my glass of water was actually a gin and tonic. Once his eyes are locked with mine, he says, "You are the doctor here, not me, Dr. Frank. Where would you like us to start?" Then just like that, his eyes are back to looking at the floor. I start to wonder if this is how he was with the other therapists who have tried working with him. I cannot tell what he wants from me. Does he want to talk to me at all, or is this just a game to him? I remember reading in quite a few of the articles I found that he did enjoy playing games when he was a boy. Perhaps we have just started a game of cat and mouse, but am I the cat or am I the mouse?

It is my turn to refill my water glass. The ice in the ice bin has melted completely now, so I fill the glass with room-temperature water, which I will not be drinking anyway. I just wanted a minute to gather my thoughts before I responded to him again. I have never felt so unprepared for a session before, even after all the reading I did last night. He is different from any patient I have had before, and I cannot even decide if that is a good or a bad thing.

Once I am done filling my glass, I walk back to my chair, sit down, and proceed to put my glass back on the table. I notice that as I bend over to put the glass down, he watches me; he is waiting to see if I will put the glass back on the ring of water on the table as he did. I contemplate putting it in a different spot on the table, but I think that may have a very negative affect on him for one reason or another, so I place it directly on the ring. He seems pleased with that decision and allows just the slightest hint of a smile to hit his lips.

6

BRYANT

Could he hear me? Is that why he put the glass back on the water ring? I could swear I was talking to myself. I was sure he was going to put it down somewhere else. Then, just as I was screaming to myself, *Please put it back in the same place you picked it up from,* he hesitated and redirected his aim right for the ring. I am again very impressed by you, Dr. Frank.

Though he has impressed me a few times already, I am not sure what to make of Dr. Frank just yet. For some reason, he seems unsure of himself. I see all his degrees and awards on the walls, so he must know what he is doing. He is not like the others I have been stuck with, that is for sure. He may really want to help me and not just get a paycheck or make the front page of the local newspaper for working with the boy. I wonder if he likes playing games.

Dr. Frank is the one who should be asking the questions, but he does not seem to know where to start, so I indulge him. "Have you ever heard of the game called three monkeys, Dr. Frank?" I ask him. He looks at me with a strange look on his face, then he replies, "I don't think I have ever heard of that game. How do you play it?" Is he serious right now. He has never heard of three monkeys? I thought every child has played it before. What kind of childhood did he have?

We are skipping ahead in the story if we start here, but we can always go back. If Dr. Frank wants to know the whole story, I may need help getting us there, which is why I want to make sure he knows the rules for playing three monkeys. I cannot tell if he really does not know how to play or if he is testing me to see if I really know the rules. Trust me, Dr. Frank, I know how to play three monkeys very well. However, I am not very good at playing hide-and-seek. I suspect you will find that out for yourself soon enough.

"Well, you see, Dr. Frank, we need three people to play, so unfortunately we will not be able to play today, but I can explain the rules to you. Then one day if we find another friend, we can all play together." I think Dr. Frank would like that. He seems like the game-playing type. I wonder if he has lots of friends. I bet he does. I wish I had lots of friends. I make friends pretty easily. Unfortunately, they never seem to stick around for very long.

"The rules are fairly simple, Dr. Frank. There are always three monkeys, which all have a different secret power. One of them has the power to not be able to see any evil that happens. One of them has the power to not be able to hear any evil that happens, and the third one has the power to not be able to speak about any evil that happens. When we do get to play, I want to be the speak-no-evil monkey. I hope that is okay with you, Dr. Frank. I am always the speak-no-evil one. I am very good at it. That would leave you with either the hear-no-evil monkey or the see-no-evil monkey. Our new friend, when we find one, would be stuck with whichever one you do not want to be." Explaining this to Dr. Frank is starting to bring back a lot of memories that I have tried extremely hard to forget. It is making me think of my two friends who vanished without even saying goodbye or telling me where they were going. It is making me miss them again.

Dr. Frank still has that confused look on his face. Is he not paying attention to me? He has been writing in his notebook quite a bit, but he is not saying very much. Then he looks up from his notebook and just says "Go on," so I do. "Once we all choose the monkey we are going to be, we take turns helping each other work through different, sometimes difficult situations, which are too bad to go through alone. Sometimes it is more fun to play when we mix it together with a good round of hide-and-seek." Surely, he must know how to play hide-and-seek. Everyone has played hide-and-seek at least once in their lifetime. I do not think he is understanding the rules. He looks perplexed now instead of just confused. It will be easier to explain it to him once we make another friend.

I look over at the clock on the wall and notice we are five minutes past our ending time. Dr. Frank has not seemed to notice. I want so badly to see what he has been writing down in his notebook. Is he writing bad things about me? Does he think I am crazy like all the others have? Is he going to give up on me too? Please help me, Dr. Frank. I need you to set me free once and for all, no matter what it takes.

CHAPTER

7

DR. FRANK

I notice his eyes have wandered over my head and realize he must be looking at the clock. I have been so intrigued by this three-monkey game that I did not even realize our session was supposed to have ended already. I have had some patients tell me some far-out stories before, but I have to say, my interest is beyond piqued with the rules to this game. I am pretty certain he is explaining his coping mechanism from his childhood to me, but again I do not want to push him this early on. I am going to continue to go at his pace, which may well be faster than the pace I was expecting. I think he is truly ready to open up to me and, hopefully, hold nothing back, a therapist's dream come true.

I hate to stop the session, but I can hear my buzzer going off to let me know my next patient has arrived. He hears it too, and he starts looking around the room, unsure what it is. Sounds can also sometimes be triggers for patients, so just in case this is one for him, I end the session. "Well, Bryant, that sound is letting me know my next patient is ready for me, so unfortunately we will have to stop here for today. It was a pleasure meeting you, and I am looking forward to our next session. I hope you are too."

I stand up and walk toward the door. I can hear the sounds of him also getting up from his chair, but his footsteps seem to be going away from me instead of toward me. Before I open the door, I turn around, and I see him standing at the window again.

In my line of work, it is often said that being able to feel empathy for your patients can be a positive and a negative thing. It is never a good idea to let oneself get emotionally attached to your patients, no matter what you are treating them for. You should always be professional and never cross any lines that could cause any kind of harm to your patients be it physical or emotional. Although I do understand the rationale behind this, I have at times found it very difficult to adhere to it.

I stand there with my hand on the doorknob and just observe the way he is standing there. He has both of his hands up against the pane of glass, as if he wants to reach right through it and be free. I instantly start to feel the empathy that I knew I would feel the first time I looked into his eyes. I may not be able to read his face and know what he is thinking, but I can absolutely tell that he is not a bad person; he is not the monster that so many reporters have called him. He was not born this way; he was made to be this way.

"Time to go, Bryant. They are waiting for you downstairs. I will see you again next week at the same time." He turns around and starts walking toward me. His eyes are again looking down at the floor. As he gets closer to me, I stick my hand out for him to shake, and I am very happy that he does the same. "It was very nice meeting you, Dr. Frank," he says in a very low somber voice as he shakes my hand. Then without another word, he is gone.

Before I let my next patient in, I need a minute to work through everything that was said in our session. Most therapists these days use recorders for their sessions, but I prefer writing it down initially and then recording it later when I am alone. I have tried recording my sessions before, but I found that I was often rushing the session and missing some things the patient was telling me that I could have followed up on there and then. When I take the time to take notes, I am focusing more on what they are telling me, and therefore I typically do not miss a thing.

I have some homework to do over the next week. I need to be much more prepared for our next session. One of the first things I will be looking up is this three-monkey game. I have heard of the three wise monkeys from Japan, I believe, but I have never heard of it as a game people play. Is this something he made up himself, or was this also taught to him? If so, by whom?

8

BRYANT

Being off my medications is having some strange effects on me that I do not like very much. I have not been sleeping very well at all, which is leaving me drowsy all day long. I am also hungry all the time. I am going to be putting on some major weight eating the way I have been. Luckily there is a gym here that I get to use any day I want to so long as I have supervision to make sure I do not hurt myself. It is like having my own personal trainer. It is not all bad though, I have made some new friends! I cannot wait to tell Dr. Frank about them. I am really bad with names, so I cannot remember what they are yet. In some ways they remind me of my best friends from when I was younger. Their names I will never forget. They were identical twins. The boy's name is Mikey, and the girl's name is Nicki. I think for now I will call my new friends Michael and Nicole to make it easier for me to remember.

Maybe I will be able to bring them along with me to one of my sessions with Dr. Frank. I really think he will like them when he gets to meet them. I wish he could have met Mikey and Nicki; he definitely would have liked them. I think I will tell Dr. Frank about them also during our next session. Maybe he can help me find out what happened to them. I hope they are okay.

Truth be told, Nicki could be sort of mean sometimes, and man, did she have a foul mouth on her! If it was not for Mikey, I probably would have never become friends with Nicki. I met Mikey first, and then he started bringing Nicki along with him, and she grew on me. Besides, we needed Nicki there to play the three-monkey game with us. She would always get angry because she would be stuck with the see-no-evil monkey, which would just give her another reason to swear at us. When I think back on it now, did she really have it that bad not being able to see any evil? Trust me, there are much worse things. Sadly, whoever created the game somehow overlooked the feel-no-evil monkey. That is the one I would have wanted to be every day of my life that I lived with my parents.

I have decided that I like Dr. Frank. He seems like a nice man. I have not, however, decided if I can trust him yet. I have a very hard time trusting anyone at all. I will see what happens when I tell him about my friends from when I was young and about my new friends I have made now. I hope he does not get jealous because I have so many friends, which would not be a good thing. I wonder if he wants to be my friend too.

There is one thing I know for sure: Michael and Nicole are really good at playing hide-and-seek. It has been a long time since I have played, and I was never really good at it before, but I am definitely worse at it now. It takes me forever to find them when it is their turns to hide. Maybe Dr. Frank can teach me some tricks on how to find them quicker. We started playing yesterday, and I still have not found them yet. *Come out, come out, wherever you are.* I know they are here somewhere because every once in a while I can hear one of them or smell one of them, I just cannot tell where it is coming from.

What if I never find them? Will they just give up and show themselves? I sure hope so, or I will not be able to introduce them to Dr. Frank. Then he will think I am just making them up to trick him into thinking I have a lot of friends. I don't want him to think I am lying to him like my mom always did. *Hush my little monkey, don't say a word.* Where did that come from? Was that Nicole? How does she know my mother used to sing that to me all the time?

CHAPTER

9

DR. FRANK

After everything that happened during our first session, I was very disappointed when our next two sessions were cancelled because of Bryant not being stable enough to make them. He started having some bad withdrawal side effects from stopping his medications. His main doctor at the facility he has been a patient at for the last almost twenty years has suggested that instead of Bryant coming to my office that perhaps I should come to him. He thinks it may also be helpful if he is in surroundings where he is more comfortable. I am not convinced he is even remotely comfortable with his surroundings, but I am willing to give it a try, especially if it is the only way I get to have another session with him.

I arrive at the facility fifteen minutes early, so I can get situated before they bring Bryant to our assigned meeting room. The room is nothing like my office. All there is in the room are two uncomfortable old folding chairs and a beat-up small table for us to sit at. There is no decor at all and definitely no windows to see any kind of view. It is one of the coldest rooms I have ever been in, and I do not mean temperaturewise.

I am very anxious to see Bryant again. I hope he is feeling better today. I do not want to be responsible for him hurting himself, or anyone else for that matter, by stopping his medications. I requested a pitcher of water with some ice, which one of the orderlies brings in right before Bryant arrives. When he walks in, I immediately notice that he is dressed in his hospital gown instead of jeans and a shirt like he was the last time I saw him. I do not know if this is by his choice or his doctor's choice, but it makes me feel uncomfortable for some reason, which may be related to a feeling of guilt.

He walks in and immediately heads for the chair, facing the door just as he did in my office. I do pay attention to these things. As he settles into his chair, I pour us both a glass of water with a few ice cubes each. I put one of the glasses down in front of him and settle into my chair the best I can. I am a bit shocked when I look over at him, and he is actually looking at me instead of the floor or the table. He must be ready to talk, so I do not waste a single minute of our hour together. I start right in, "I heard you have not been feeling well. Are you feeling better today?" He does not even hesitate, "I am feeling much better today, Dr. Frank. How are you feeling?" I need to make a decision right now before either of us say another word. I need to decide how I want this session to go. During our first session, I let him lead the way; it went very well, even better than I had anticipated. But I can already tell there is a change in his personality today. He is not shying away from me like he did last time. He is much more present and almost assertive with the tone of his voice. I may have my hands full today.

"I am feeling good today as well," I reply. I decide in that second that today I need to be in charge, so I continue before he has a chance to. "I was reviewing my notes from our first session, and I was hoping we could continue our talk about the three-monkey game. I have some follow-up questions for you."

To my surprise, his blue eyes light up, and he lets a smile take over his face. The best way I can explain it is the way a child reacts when they are handed an ice cream cone. Then it hits me just like that, as if someone just snapped their fingers very loudly in my ear. He is not the twenty-eight-year-old Bryant I met in my office; he is the nine-year-old Bryant who loved playing the three-monkey game. *Holy shit!*

Maybe his doctor was onto something. Maybe being here in a place he has been for so long will help him to be more relaxed and comfortable. I had not even thought of that before. I always believed that getting the patient out of the place they felt trapped in would help them be more receptive to my helping them. On the other hand, maybe the differences I am seeing is due to the medications being completely out of his system now. That makes more sense to me. Either way, I have a strong feeling this is going to be a very productive session today. I take a drink of my water and wait for his reply.

10

BRYANT

"I am so sorry I was not able to make our last two sessions Dr. Frank. I hope you are not mad at me. We sure can talk more about the three-monkey game if you want to, but would it be okay with you if I tell you my really good news first?" I have been so excited about telling Dr. Frank about my new friends even though they are still hiding from me, which is not very nice of them. I really hope he will believe me even though he cannot meet them today.

Dr. Frank looks more serious today than he did during our first session. "I'll tell you what," he says, "you can tell me your good news as long as we talk about the three-monkey game right after that. How does that sound to you?" He sounds more like my doctor today than he does my friend, and he did not even shake my hand.

"That sounds good to me, Dr. Frank," I say. "My good news is that I made some new friends. I have been playing hide-and-seek with them the last couple of days. But either they are really good at hiding or I am a really bad seeker because I can-not find them anywhere. I wanted you to meet at least one of them today so we could play the three-monkey game together.

That way you would be able to understand the rules better. I can't remember their names right now, but I call them Michael and Nicole because they remind me of my best friends I had when I was nine, and their names were Mikey and Nicki."

I take a drink of my water while it is still a little cold before I ask Dr. Frank my really important question. "I was wondering if you could help me figure out how to find my friends when they are hiding so well. Do you have any secret ways of making them come out of hiding?" I hope it was okay to ask him about that. I do not know who else I could ask. He said he wants to help me, and I could sure use some help with being a better seeker.

Dr. Frank says, "I will make you a deal, Bryant. I will help you figure out how to find your friends quicker once we finish talking about the three-monkey game. I really want to know more about the game before our session ends today." He does not seem very friendly to me today. I sure hope he is not upset with me because I made new friends.

"That sounds like a good deal to me, Dr. Frank. What else would you like to know about the game? I really wish we could play today." Does he want to ask me more questions about the game so he can play it with his other friends instead of me? That would not be very nice of him. He probably just wants to know more about it now so that he will be ready when we get to play it together. I bet that is it.

"I am sorry we cannot play it today too, Bryant. But don't worry, I think we will be able to play it really soon. I was wondering if you could tell me when the first time you played it was and who you played it with. Also, who taught you how to play it? Or did you make it up yourself?"

I really hope Dr. Frank means it when he says we will be able to play soon. I do not know if Michael and Nicole are going to like the game. Nicole is sort of mean like Nicki was, so she might not like playing it with Michael and me, which will really stink.

"I guess it was my mom that initially taught me how to play when I was about eight years old. Me and my mom were close, really close, you could say, when I was a little boy. Anyway, the older I got, the more she started to dislike me. I would tell her my secrets, and she would always call me a liar and punish me. That is how I became the speak-no-evil monkey, from my mom. 'Hush, my little monkey, don't say a word.' I guess she thought if I did not speak of the evil, it meant it never happened. But trust me, Dr. Frank, it did happen. She wanted me to be all three of the monkeys at the same time, but I was too young to do that, which would make her even madder at me. Then one day I met Mikey. He was my best friend I was talking about earlier. I told him about how mad my mom would get at me because I could not be all three of the monkeys at the same time and how she would punish me, so he offered to be one of the monkeys for me. He always liked to be the hear-no-evil one. He has an identical twin sister, Nicki, who he eventually talked into playing with us one night when things got too bad for just the two of us. She became the see-no-evil monkey. You see, Dr. Frank, once Mikey and Nicki became my best friends, I did not have to be all three monkeys anymore. They were there to help me through what I could not have gone through by myself. We can talk about my mom and my dad more later if you want to, Dr. Frank."

11

DR. FRANK

"Flabbergasted," that is the word that comes to my mind to describe how I am feeling right now. After everything I have heard from previous patients through the years, there is not much they can tell me that will leave me feeling lost for words. It is not just the things that Bryant says; it is also the tone he uses when he says them. I am sitting directly across from him. He is less than three feet away from me. He is a handsome man with amazing blue eyes. He is also in great physical shape. Yet if I was blindfolded, I would swear I was listening to a child telling me his story. It is possible I may be misunderstanding what he just explained to me, but if I am correct, then he just told me that his mother was abusing him herself or knew he was being abused by someone else, and she expected him to pretend to be monkeys with different special powers to make it all okay. How do I wrap my head around all of that? I need to help this man if it is the last thing I ever do.

"Bryant, thank you so much for sharing all of that with me. I believe I know how to play the game now. I also want to say that I am so sorry your mom treated you so badly. I noticed you did not talk about your dad much. I hope he was much nicer to you." In most cases I have seen, it is the father who is the abuser, but from what he is telling me so far, it sounds like it was his mother. Though this is rare, it is not unheard of.

It looks like he is deep in thought after my last comment. I wonder what he is thinking about. I wish I could read his mind, never mind his face. What is going on in there? I then notice that my own mind is working a little overtime also. I am mentally scanning all the articles I found and printed, looking for anything that was said about his father. Was he just an innocent bystander in all of this who for some reason ended up dead right next to his wife with no just cause? I find that very hard to believe, especially considering the way his body was left. I am also finding it even harder to believe that this gentle, timid, quiet man could be capable of what so many people say or believe he did.

"Bryant, I was wondering if you would like to talk about your mom and dad today, or would you rather wait until our next session?" Right as I finish asking him that question, I remember I told him I would help him come up with a way to find his friends quicker. I doubt very much he has forgotten that. At this point it seems to be his biggest concern. We have much more serious things to talk about, but I do not want him to think I lied to him like so many other people in his life have.

He seems to have gathered his thoughts. He grabs his glass of water and takes a big long drink from it before making sure to place it right back in the same spot he picked it up from. I wonder if he got that behavior from his mother too. He then refocuses back on me and says, "I would like to talk about my mom and dad next time, Dr. Frank. You said you would help me become a better seeker today, and I know you would not lie to me. Speak no evil, as my mom would say to me."

His mind may be all over the place, but he did not forget I said that, did he? I can do this; I just need to take baby steps to make sure he can handle it. "Sounds like a good idea, Bryant. That way we can spend all of our next session focused on just your mom and dad. Okay, so I have found that sometimes when you play hide-and-seek and you are having a hard time finding your friends' hiding places, it can be helpful to tease them a little bit to get them to want to come out. It does not work all the time, but maybe you could give it a try."

I cannot tell if he is understanding what I am trying to tell him. He has sort of a puzzled look on his face. Let me take one more step to get him there. "Suppose you and I were playing hide-and-seek, and I was hidden so good you would never find me, but you knew I love brownies. If you put some brownies in the oven and the smell of them baking drifted through the air to where I was hiding, I may give up my hiding place to join you for a brownie. Does that make sense?"

His eyes light up again, and he starts to giggle a bit. "I love brownies too, Dr. Frank. I would come out of my hiding place if I could smell you baking brownies. That makes a lot of sense to me. Do you think you could bake some brownies for me, Dr. Frank, or should I ask my other doctor to bake me some so I can get my friends to come out of hiding?"

It takes all the self-control I have in me to not burst out laughing. Like I said, baby steps, the tiniest baby steps possible. Let me try again, "I was only using baking brownies as an example of how you could get me out of my hiding place because I love brownies. You will have to find out what your other friends like that would make them want to come out of their hiding places. Find a way to tease them or tempt them enough to give up those great hiding places."

The next thing I hear is the buzzer on my phone alerting me our hour is up. He hears it too, and his smile suddenly disappears. He knows what it means this time. "I will try to find out what my new friends like, Dr. Frank. I hope it is brownies.

Maybe next time you can meet one of them," he says as he gets up out of his very uncomfortable chair and heads for the door. Until we meet again.

C H A P T E R

12

BRYANT

Dr. Frank might be onto something with his idea about how I can become a better seeker. I just need to figure out something I can do or say to Michael and Nicole that will make them willing to give up their hiding places. I think it will be easier for me to get Michael's attention after some of the things he has told me about himself. I do not really want to betray his trust by using things he has confided to me to lure him out of hiding, but I just might have to. It will be more difficult with Nicole, considering I do not think she likes me very much. I may have to be a little more conniving with her. I first started seeing the two of them hanging around here and there shortly after Dr. Frank had my doctor stop my medications.

There is something strange about Michael and Nicole that I cannot quite put my finger on just yet. You know when you meet someone for the first time, and you get the feeling that you know them from somewhere, but you just cannot remember where? That is how I am when I see either of them. I have not been able to see the two of them together yet. I am not even sure if they know each other, though I must admit they do look a lot alike. Wouldn't it be funny if they were twins too? That would be very helpful in my quest. I could let Nicole think something is wrong with Michael to get her to come out. Yes, Dr. Frank, you may really be onto something here.

I am having a hard time trying to remember anything I know about Nicole that may have an important element I could use to get her attention. I do remember that she drinks rosé wine all the time. I also know she listens to 99.9 FM on the radio while she is getting ready to go out to bars pretty much every Friday night. Maybe there is something related to rosé wine or the radio or even bars I can use. I did not mention it to Dr. Frank because I do not know him well enough to know how he would have reacted, but I do know that Michael is gay, and he models, mostly only in his underwear. He also works out a lot at the gym. I am sure I can think of some way to get to him.

I think I am having a hard time focusing on Michael and Nicole because my mind keeps going back to my childhood ever since Dr. Frank said he wants us to talk about my mom and dad in our next session. I keep seeing small bits and pieces of memories going pretty far back. There was a time from when I was around nine years old in which I have a lot of memory losses. That was right around the time that I was seeing Mikey and Nicki pretty much every day, and we would play the three-monkey game and hide-and-seek. I guess I was just having too much fun to form lasting memories. I sure wish Dr. Frank could find them for me. They would be able to help me remember more of what was happening during that year so I could tell Dr. Frank about it. Nobody likes a story with a lot of holes in it.

I have not talked about my parents with anyone since the day they both died. The other therapists before Dr. Frank all tried to get me to talk, but I did not say a word. I also did not say anything to the reporters or the lawyers or the judge. Would it have mattered anyway? Who was going to believe that

I, a nine-year-old boy whose parents were both murdered, was innocent after the way they found the three of us? So I have been silent all these years until now.

I sure hope Dr. Frank will still want to be my friend after he hears everything that I have to tell him about my mom and dad and the three monkeys. I wonder if he will believe me. Maybe someday I will even tell him my real name.

CHAPTER

13

DR. FRANK

My last session with Bryant was quite an exciting one. Any doubts that I may have had about him being ready to open up and share his story with me have gone out the window, leading his way to freedom. Therapy does not typically move along this quickly, which is also telling me that he is more than ready to let me into his private world. I just hope I am as ready for it as he seems. I am trying so hard to not let myself get emotionally attached to him, but it has not been easy. I already know some of the things he is going to be telling me in our next session from what I have heard and read over the last almost twenty years, and none of it is good. I do also have to keep reminding myself that he was found guilty of murdering his own parents in a court of law. I just do not see how that could be possible. Our next couple of sessions are going to be extremely personal and emotional for him. I hope I am doing the right thing.

I have noticed he keeps bringing up his two friends, Mikey and Nicki, from right around the time his parents died. Last night I was scanning all the articles again, and I did not see either of their names mentioned anywhere. I will need to ask him some follow-up questions about them, especially if he wants me to try to find them for him. After so many years, they could be anywhere. Maybe he at least remembers their last name so I have some way to start my search. Hopefully it will not be a complete waste of my time.

I guess I should have shown more interest in what he was telling me about making new friends. To be honest, I just wanted him to start telling me about his mother and father, but he was so excited to tell me about his friends that I did not want to upset him by just changing the subject on him. All I can remember is that he does not even know their real names, so he calls them Michael and Nicole, and they like to hide on him for hours, if not days, at a time. Not quite sure how that is even possible given where he lives. They must be new patients if he has only just started being friends with them recently. I do not think I would consider them friends due to the way they are treating him, they do not seem to play nicely. I will need to follow up with him on them too.

To be as prepared as I possibly can be for our next session, I have been doing as much research as I can on his mother and father. Unfortunately, there is not very much information available about them before the time of their deaths. I know that his father's name was Paul, and his mother's name was Janet. They were married in 1990 when they were twenty-five and twenty-three years old respectively. At the time of their deaths in 2001, they were only in their early to midthirties. From what I have found, it looks like his father was some sort of construction worker, and his mother was a stay-at-home mom. They never had any other children. They were renting the house they lived and died in. I also found a few disorderly conduct complaints regarding Paul, all related to excessive drinking. It is odd that I did not find any records of calls or complaints to do with any kind of abuse issues related to Janet or Bryant.

The last thing I do before calling it a night is something I will regret very quickly. I take out the folder I have that includes copies of all the photos that were taken the night of the murders. They are very gruesome to look at and will most likely give me nightmares. I think it will be helpful to study the photos and memorize as many of the details as I can before hearing what Bryant has to say. I am hopeful that he is going to tell me the true story of what happened, but if he starts telling me lies, hopefully, I will know by comparing what he tells me to what I can see in the photos. As I look through the photos, I am shocked by how much blood there was at the scene. I realize two people lost their lives that night, but my god, there is blood everywhere.

The very last photo is the one that will be stuck in my head for a very long time. I am guessing it was one of the very first ones that were taken when the cops showed up. It is a photo of a nine-year-old Bryant sitting like an Indian, almost completely covered in blood with a knife in his hand. His face looks completely blank, especially those beautiful blue eyes. What exactly was going on inside that house? Do I really want to know? Do I really want to make Bryant remember what he has worked so hard to forget? I hope it is worth it in the end.

14

BRYANT

I cannot wait to see Dr. Frank again and tell him more about Michael and Nicole. I think he will be very happy with the progress I am making thanks to his advice. I have been a little more confused than usual lately. Strange things started happening. I am not completely positive, but I think Michael and Nicole have been sneaking into my place when I am not there. I started finding things that do not belong to me, and sometimes I can smell things that I should not be smelling. I do have to admit, the first time I smelled just the faintest hint of Chanel No. 5 on my bedsheets, it really freaked me out. I have not smelled that scent in almost twenty years. That was the perfume that my mom wore every day. I think it is Michael and Nicole teasing me because I am so bad at finding their hiding places. It is like they are saying, "We are right here under your nose, and you still cannot find us."

But thanks to Dr. Frank's great trick, which I started using this last week, I think I may have found a way to beat them at their own game. I knew from the things that Michael has told me that he goes to the gym a lot, so I started going more often than I had, and one of the times that I went, he actually showed up too. I didn't want him to know that I had seen him, so I snuck out as quick as I could. No need for him to think I am following him around like I have no other friends. It is very possible that he might be attracted to me, so I may be able to use that to get him to come out of hiding to meet Dr. Frank one day.

As for Nicole, I remembered about her listening to the radio on Friday nights, so I have started talking to her while she has the radio on. So far, she has not figured out that it is me. I have even given her fashion advice and tips, though she does not listen to what I tell her. I do not think she has figured out that it is her I am talking to directly. Once I am ready for Dr. Frank to meet her, I will start calling her by her name to get her full attention, which will hopefully get her to come out of hiding like Dr. Frank said it could.

It is all coming together nicely. Once they get to know me better, maybe they will want to play the three-monkey game with me instead of just hide-and-seek all the time. They never let me be one of the ones that gets to hide. I am always the seeker, which is not as much fun. I wonder where they are right now.

Darn it, I forgot I told Dr. Frank we will spend the next session talking about my mom and dad. The two people in the world who should have never been allowed to have any children. Lucky me. I guess I will have to wait for another session to talk about Michael and Nicole. Maybe by then I will have been able to get them to give up their hiding places, and they can meet Dr. Frank. I hope they all get along. Nicole can be kind of mean at times, but Dr. Frank is so nice that maybe she will be nice back to him. I sure hope she does not swear at him like she does to almost everyone else, and hopefully she will not be drunk on rosé wine.

I have also been trying really hard to remember more about what happened around the time my parents died so I will be ready for the questions Dr. Frank might ask me. Unfortunately, I still have lots of blank spaces that I have not been able to fill no matter how hard I try. If Dr. Frank could find and talk to Mikey and Nicki, they might be able to fill in some of the blanks that I cannot. I hope he doesn't think I am lying to him when I tell him how much of my memory is missing. I have no reason to lie to him, and lying leads to being punished. I have been punished enough in my lifetime already.

15

DR. FRANK

Today is the big day, the day I have been anxiously waiting a long time for. I arrive fifteen minutes early again at the facility that Bryant has called home for two-thirds of his life, so I have enough time to get myself situated before they bring him in. I do not want to waste a single minute of this session. I am as prepared as I possibly can be. I hope he does not change his mind about talking about his parents today. I have more than enough questions ready to ask him to fill the entire hour. I have even decided that I am going to record this session instead of taking notes to keep it moving along quicker. I do not want our hour to be up and still have unanswered questions, though I am pretty sure there will always be more questions to ask in a case like this one.

They bring him into our meeting room, the same one as last time, at exactly 9:00 a.m. He is again dressed in his hospital gown, but he looks like he is in a better mood today. I stand up and shake his hand, which brings a smile to his face. We both take our seats, and for just a moment, instead of seeing the man sitting right across from me, I see a nine-year-old boy covered in blood with the knife still in his hand. Am I sitting three feet away from a stone-cold killer?

I start in right away. "As we discussed in our last session, Bryant, I would like to spend our time together today talking about your mom and dad. To get us started, I am hoping you will share with me the earliest memory you have of you and your mom or dad. It does not matter if it is good or bad, just the earliest you can think of." I sure hope this does not backfire on me.

His eye contact is focused on me, which should mean he is ready to reply, and then he does. "I will tell you everything I can remember, Dr. Frank, but there are lots of times that I have no memories at all from when I was growing up. My memories are sort of in blocks of time. It is sometimes hard for me to put them in the correct order. They seem to jump around all over the place, but I will do the best I can for you. I can tell you, when I was really young, my mom loved me so much. She spoiled me rotten all the time. She never wanted me out of her sight. She gave me anything I wanted. My mom and my dad would get into fights over me. My dad would tell my mom she was babying me too much and that I would grow up to be a homosexual if she did not let me be the boy I was born to be. The fighting went on and on for a long time. Then one day it got even worse when my dad came home from work early and walked in on me and my mom during our private time. I think I was eight years old when that happened." Then he pauses, leaving me hanging. Is he waiting for me to ask him what he means by "private time"? Is he making sure I am listening to him considering I am taping our session for the first time?

The suspense is killing me, so I ask what needs to be asked. "What exactly did your dad walk in on during your private time with your mom, Bryant?" A part of me feels awful for making him talk about these horrible things that happened to him, but if I don't ask, he may not tell me, and that will not do him any good at all. I will not be able to help him if I do not know the whole true story.

"Like I mentioned before, Dr. Frank, I am not good with putting my memories in order, so I cannot tell you exactly when we started having our private times together, but I think they started as soon as I was born. I do not know why my dad was so angry when he walked in on us, but he just started screaming at both of us like we were doing something wrong. I guess my mom never told him that we never stopped doing it every day. My mom always told me that it was our private time and how special it was for us to be so close to each other. I had no idea that it was not normal for a mom to breastfeed her child until he was almost nine years old."

Did he just say what I think he said? His mother breastfed him from when he was born until he was eight or nine years old. I have never heard of a mother doing that before. Maybe to the age of two or three, but even that is pushing it. That gives a whole new meaning to being close to your mother. No wonder his father was so angry.

"After my dad caught us, things got so much worse for all of us. It was like my mom changed overnight. She went from loving me to hating me in a matter of twenty-four hours. She no longer spoiled me or gave me anything I wanted. It was like she blamed me for my dad walking in on us. She would punish me all the time. It did not matter if I did anything to deserve it or not. Sometimes she would put a chair in the corner of the room, facing the wall, and she would tie me to the chair. She would leave me sitting there for hours at a time. I would cry and beg her to untie me, but she was great at tuning me out. I wet my pants more times than I can count while being tied to that chair. To mix it up, sometimes she would shove me into the closet and lock me in there in the pitch-black, with nothing to eat or drink for hours. I would usually just cry until I had no tears left."

He pauses again, and I can see that his beautiful blue eyes are filled with tears that he is trying so hard to hold back. Then he looks directly at me, and he asks, "Do you think we can get some water, Dr. Frank? I am really thirsty." I cannot believe I forgot to have them bring us some water. It is not like I can tell him no, can I? "Of course, we can. Let me call someone to get us some." I use my cell phone to call the front desk and ask to have a pitcher of water brought to our room. I can tell by looking at him that he is not saying another word to me until he gets his water. They better hurry up!

16

BRYANT

I cannot tell if Dr. Frank is believing what I am telling him about my mom and dad or not. I am trying really hard to remember everything I can, but after all these years of trying to not remember, it is even more scrambled in my mind. There are parts I will never forget, but with so many missing pieces, I find it hard to put the ones that I do have in the correct order. I asked for some water because I needed a minute to get myself ready for what I am going to tell Dr. Frank next. I hope he will not hate me once he hears it.

They bring the water in with two glasses. Dr. Frank fills both glasses and slides one across the table to me. I take a nice big gulp, swallow it down, then take another drink before putting the glass down on the table. Dr. Frank does not drink his at all. He just sits there looking at me, patiently waiting for me to continue. I take a deep breath and pick up where I left off.

"My dad started drinking even more after he walked in on me and my mom's private time. Some days he would not come home at all. I remember a few times the police had been called because he was being disorderly, I think they called it. He and my mom were hardly even speaking to each other. Most of the time when they did, it was screaming instead of talking. It was not a happy house, Dr. Frank. I was scared all the time."

I start to feel my throat go dry again when I try to tell Dr. Frank what happened next. I have never told anyone about this before, and I do not know if he will believe me, but I am going to tell him anyway. I take another drink of water, and as I go to put the glass back down, I notice this time there is a ring of water on the table, so I make sure to put the glass directly over it. I notice Dr. Frank is watching me as I do this, and I can tell he wants to ask me about it, but he doesn't.

"Do you remember I mentioned my two friends who vanished on me, Mikey and Nicki?" I ask Dr. Frank, to which he just nods, as if he does not want to interrupt my thought process. "I am not sure when I first met them, but I think it was a couple of months before my parents died. That was the same time when my memory losses started happening more often, and it was also the time when things started happening with my dad that should never have happened." Can I really go through with this? Can I tell Dr. Frank what my dad made me do? I know he is going to hate me. He is not going to want to be my friend anymore.

"A couple of nights before I met Mikey, my mom had punished me because she did not like the way I looked at her. She tied me to the chair, but this time she went to bed without untying me. I somehow ended up falling asleep while still tied to the chair. My dad came home really late and really drunk that night. He was banging into things, which woke me up. He had not turned on any lights, so he did not even see me until I called out to him to untie me." I still wonder to this day if my parents would still be alive if I had managed to sleep through the night.

"My dad came over to where I was and started laughing at me. 'What has that crazy bitch been doing to you now, boy?' he said to me in a very slurred voice. He grabbed hold of the chair and turned it around so that I was facing him. Then the real nightmare began. 'If you like sucking on your mommy's breast so much, I have something for you to suck on too,' he said as he undid the zipper of his jeans. I did not understand what he was talking about or why he was unzipping his jeans. I had never seen my dad's penis before. He moved closer to me, and he told me to open my mouth. I have never been so scared in all my life, so I did what he told me to do. He proceeded to put his penis in my mouth and told me to suck it like I did my mother's breast. It kept getting bigger and bigger until I started to choke on it, which made me start to cry. He pulled his penis back out of my mouth, put it back into his jeans, and said, 'Don't worry, you will get used to it.' He then turned the chair back around and left me there, facing the corner, tied to the chair."

I look over at Dr. Frank, he has not taken his eyes off me for even a second. He looks completely horrified. He definitely does not want to be my friend anymore.

"The next morning, my dad left for work before my mom was out of bed. He did not even look at me or say a single word to me. He may not have remembered what he did to me the night before, he was so drunk. When my mom finally got out of bed, she acted shocked that I was still tied to the chair. She must have thought I was Houdini and would be able to untie myself, or maybe she thought my dad would have untied me. She walked over to me and finally undid the ropes that held me to that chair. The only thing she said to me was, 'That will teach you to look at your mother that way again,' and she walked away. There was so much going on in my head that morning that it felt like it was going to split open. I was starving, thirsty, sore all over from being in that chair all night, my wrists hurt from the ropes, but most of all I felt dirty from what my dad had made me do. I started praying to myself that it would never happen again. The Lord did not hear my prayers that morning,

Dr. Frank. My dad continued to abuse me in the same way every time he was home alone with me."

"It was during this time that I started seeing Mikey more often, and I told him about what was happening. He did not believe me at first. Who would believe that a dad would do things like that to his own boy? Mikey convinced me that I should tell my mom what was happening. I had been too afraid to tell her, but maybe if I did, she would make my dad stop like he stopped my private times with her."

"One morning after my dad had left for work and my mom seemed like she was actually in a good mood, I asked her if I could tell her a secret. When I was younger and my mom still loved me, I would tell her all my secrets, but that stopped when she stopped loving me. She said, 'Of course you can tell me a secret. You can tell me anything. I'm your mom.' My instincts were telling me it would be a mistake to tell her, but if there was even the slightest chance that telling her would get my dad to stop doing it, then I had to take the chance, so I did. I told her all of it, from how it started the night she left me tied in the chair to how it now happens all the time when she is not home with us. I never would have imagined her reaction being what it was in a million years. The first thing she did was pull her arm all the way back and slap me across the face as hard as she could. It almost made me fall over. I instantly began bawling my eyes out. She then grabbed me by my wrist and pulled me across the room into the bathroom. She told me to take all my clothes off. While I stripped down, she turned the shower on with the water as hot as it would go. The mirror was completely covered by the hot steam coming out of the shower before I was done undressing. Once I was completely naked, she told me to get in the shower and sit down like an Indian. The water was so hot my skin turned instantly red. If I hadn't still been crying from when she slapped me, I would have started crying then. Once I managed to get all the way into the bathtub, it took everything I had to get my body to sit down on the bottom of the tub with that extremely hot water falling on me. I was making a noise I have never heard before. It was a mix of me screaming from the hot water hitting me and the sounds of me still crying like I have never cried before."

"My mom then calmly lowered herself to the floor, grabbed the bar of soap, and shoved it into my mouth while I was still crying. It tasted so awful I almost threw up all over myself. She then looked right into my eyes and said, 'Don't you ever speak such evil about your own dad again. Lying is the devil's work.' The next thing I knew, she was running her hands through my wet hair and whispering ever so gently, 'Hush, my little monkey, don't say a word.' Then she got up off the floor, shut the shower off, and walked out of the bathroom, leaving me there alone. That was the same day Mikey introduced me to his twin sister, Nicki."

CHAPTER

17

DR. FRANK

My eyes are burning from not blinking for so long. I have not been able to take my eyes off Bryant for a second while he has been sharing all his deepest, darkest secrets and fears with me. From the way he tells it, I feel like I am there in that house with him, living his nightmare. No child should ever have to live through what his parents did to him. Not only did his mother abuse him first by making him breastfeed way past the appropriate age, but she also physically and mentally abused him. Then his father started sexually abusing him, and when he went to his mother for help, she called him a liar and washed his mouth out with soap while making him sit under scalding-hot water. It is hard for me to listen to him talk about it, never mind come to the realization that he lived through it. Now I understand why he never told anyone what happened before. He lived in fear his whole life, and to make it worse, his own parents were the ones responsible for the fear. The two people who should have been there to protect him were his torturers.

We both take a drink of water, and we both put our glasses back on the water rings, but this time I ask him about it. "Bryant, I have noticed that you always make sure to put your glass right over the ring of water it has made on the table, and I was wondering why that is." Right after I ask him, I wonder if it was a mistake. He may start to wander and not go back to telling me about his parents.

"I have been waiting for you to ask me about that, Dr. Frank. You see, we never had any really nice things in our house. We weren't poor exactly, but we were by no means rich, if you know what I mean. A lot of the furniture we had was from a secondhand store, including the dining room table that my dad had just bought the past weekend. Anyway, one day I was really bored, and I was sitting at our new dining room table, drinking a nice glass of ice-cold water. One of the times I went to put the glass back down after taking a drink, I noticed it had left a ring on the table. I decided to make a game out of it. I started moving the glass all over the table, making connecting rings like a chain. What I did not realize, was that because of the material the table was made of, the rings did not go away when they dried up. They left stains all over the table. I knew right away I was in trouble. When my mom saw all the rings on the table, she came and found me hiding in my room. All she said was, 'Wait until your father sees what you did to his new table.' I wet my pants right there and then."

"I hid in my room the entire day. I was too afraid to go anywhere near my mom. That night, my dad came home from another night of heavy drinking. My mom had waited up for him. As soon as he was in the door, I heard her say, 'Look what your son did to your new table.' The very next thing I heard was my mom go into her bedroom and close the door. She knew what she had set in motion, whether she would admit it or not, and she did not care at all."

There is a part of me that wants to tell him he can stop telling me about this horrific stuff, but I have a strong feeling that what is coming next will be a major part of this whole mess. As

I look across the table at him now, I can tell his eyes are again full of tears that he is fighting to hold in, and he looks so broken. My heart is hurting for him. I am a professional man, but I am also a warm, caring man, so I do what I think is the right thing to do. "Bryant, if this is too much for you, we can take a break now."

To my surprise, he does not take the out I offered him. "It's okay, Dr. Frank, I want to tell you the whole truth. After I heard my mom's bedroom door close, I jumped out of my bed and went to hide in my closet. I knew my dad would find me, but I had to at least try. I could hear his footsteps coming toward my door then the sound of the door opening. He did not turn on the bedroom light. There was only a little bit of light coming into the room from the hallway light for him to see by. When he realized I was not in my bed, he did not even bother to look for me. Instead he just said, 'If you do not come here right now, this will be so much worse for you. In my nine-year-old mind, I couldn't imagine how it could be any worse than what he was already making me do to him, so I did not move a muscle. I sat there in the corner of my closet as quiet as a mouse. It felt like forever before he said or did anything. I was hoping he would give up and just go away, but that is not what happened by any means."

"I could hear him start looking for me under the bed, behind the drapes, and in my toy chest. Then he opened the closet doors. He started throwing my clothes off the hangers, onto the floor, until he saw me crouched down as small as I could go in the corner. He looked right at me and said, 'Get on the fucking bed now!' I had seen my dad drunk before, and I had definitely seen him mad, but I had never heard him talk like that before. I knew I was in for it bad that night. I got up off the closet floor and made my way slowly to my bed and sat on the edge of it. He walked toward me and said, 'You really should have come out when I told you to, boy.' He started taking all his clothes off, which he had never done before in front of me. When he was completely naked, he told me to take my pajamas off, which I did. He then made me suck on his penis like he has been making me do for months now, but this time he did not finish like he had. This time, he took his penis out of my mouth and told me to lie on my stomach on the bed. This was the first time he anally raped me, Dr. Frank. It hurt so much I was screaming for him to stop, but he ignored my screams and just kept doing it until he was done. When he was finished, he picked up his clothes and just left me there, bleeding on my bed. There was no way my mom did not hear my screams, yet she did not come help me while he was raping me or after."

"The only good thing that happened that night, Dr. Frank, was that because it was so dark in my room, my dad did not notice that Mikey and Nicki were there with me. That was our first official time we played the three-monkey game. Mikey had chosen the hear-no-evil monkey, so he could not hear any of what was happening. Nicki was the see-no-evil monkey, so she could not see any of what was happening. I was the speak-no-evil monkey, which meant that no matter what, I could not speak any evil against my dad like my mom had told me. Mikey and Nicki helped me out of my bed and walked me to the bathroom. They turned on the hot water and helped me climb in the tub. I sat down like an Indian under the scalding-hot water and let it rinse all the filth and blood off me. I sat there until my whole body was pruned and beet red from the heat of the water. Then Mikey and Nicki helped me out of the tub, dried me off, walked me back to my room, and put me into my bed."

CHAPTER

18

BRYANT

For some reason I feel like a weight has been lifted off my chest. I do not have the nerve to look at Dr. Frank in the eyes. He must hate me now, and I do not want to see that look on his face. I saw the look of hate enough on my mom and dad's faces to last the rest of my life. He has not said a single word to me, another friend lost. I might as well finish telling him the rest of what I remember, which is not very much.

"After that night, my memory gets really bad, Dr. Frank. I started seeing Mikey and Nicki more and more. We would play hide-and-seek all the time, and on the nights that my dad decided he wanted to use and abuse me for his own pleasure, the three of us would play the three-monkey game. That was my life up until the night my parents died."

Dr. Frank just sits there, I can feel him staring at me, but he still says nothing. I think he wants me to continue, but I know we are almost out of time, and I really want to ask him if he has any news on Mikey and Nicki. He may not help me find them now after everything I told him, but without them, he will never know the whole story.

"Dr. Frank, I was wondering if you have had any luck finding my friends Mikey and Nicki? I will need their help to finish telling you the rest of the story about my mom and dad." It cannot hurt to ask. Dr. Frank takes a drink of his water, puts his glass back in the same place he picked it up from, and then looks at me with a very sad face.

"Bryant, we are almost out of time for today, but I wanted to talk to you about a few things before we go. First, I want to thank you for trusting me enough to share so much of your story with me, I am truly honored. Second, I want to say how very sorry I am for everything that has happened to you at the hands of your own mom and dad. Lastly, I want to make sure you know that none of what happened to you was your fault. Every bit of blame is on your mom and dad. You were an innocent child whom they abused in every way possible.

"As for your friends Mikey and Nicki, I did a little digging to try to find them for you. I went through every article I could find about your case, but strangely, neither of them was mentioned anywhere, so I have nothing to go on. I was hoping you might remember where they lived or what their last name is. Anything at all you can remember that could help me try to locate them."

It does not sound like Dr. Frank is mad at me. I think he still wants to help me even after what I told him. Maybe we really can be friends. I would really like that. Then the buzzer goes off to let us know our session is over. I did it. I finally did it. I told someone besides Mikey and Nicki about my childhood. Dr. Frank starts to get up from his chair, so I do the same. I feel so much lighter than I did when I came into this room an hour ago. Then I realize that I did not answer his last questions.

"I know our time is up, Dr. Frank, but to answer your questions, I never knew where they lived. I was always being punished, so they always came to my house. I never went to theirs. As for their last name, that one is easy, it is Hughes, Mikey and Nicki Hughes. They have the same last name as I do." I make sure I shake Dr. Frank's hand goodbye as I am led out of our meeting room and back to my place.

I did not get to talk to Dr. Frank about what has been happening with Michael and Nicole. I think he would be proud of the progress I have been making thanks to his great advice. I have started letting Michael see glimpses of me here and there, and I have been talking more directly to Nicole even without a radio on. Though I have told Dr. Frank most of what happened to me, there are some things that I have not shared with him yet. I am not sure he would understand or even believe me. It is not easy to completely trust anyone, never mind when he is your therapist. I am afraid of what his reaction will be when I tell him about what happens in my private world.

When my nightmare began with my parents and I met Mikey and Nicki, not only did we play hide-and-seek and the three-monkey game together, we also created out own little private world that no one else was allowed into. Truth be told, Mikey and Nicki started it, and luckily, they invited me in. It was the safest place in the world. No one could hurt us with their words or their hands. We could be anyone we wanted to be, do anything we wanted to do, and go anywhere we wanted to go. We did not need anyone's permission for anything, and we never got punished. It was the best part of my childhood.

Since I have been off my medications, I decided to create my own new private world. When I am in my room that was assigned to me almost twenty years ago, I am not the broken, sad, depressed little boy. Instead I am a well-educated, professional man who lives in a very nice condo and runs his own private investigating company out of his home office. I am a health nut who works out almost daily and doesn't drink or smoke. You see, when I am in my small ten-foot by ten-foot room, I am who I could be, should be, would be if it had not been for my parents destroying my life, the very life they created.

I have become suspicious that Michael and Nicole have been sneaking into my place without permission. I need to know more about them before I would even consider inviting them in. I have been trying to come up with a plan to get the three of us together so I can ask them if they have indeed been letting themselves in and doing as they please when I am not here. Maybe I should try to get them to show up during my next session with Dr. Frank just in case it does not go well. Of course, if they do not show up, he may think I am making them up to try to impress him with my new friends. Hopefully, a lot of unanswered questions will be answered this weekend.

PRIVATE WORLD

CHAPTER

19

BRYANT

As I gaze over at the alarm clock on my nightstand which reads 5:32 a.m., I cannot help but think, am I the only person who wakes up in the morning and has no memory of the night before? This has been happening to me more and more lately.

After hitting the snooze button three times, I finally decide I need to get up and start my day, knowing that I most likely won't remember at least part of it tomorrow. As a single twenty-eight-year-old man living alone, I do enjoy being able to do as I please in pretty much every aspect of my life. I can eat whatever I want, whenever I want. I can be as social or antisocial as I choose. I can watch whatever crap television show I want to watch without being judged for it. There is nothing like the single life.

I pride myself on living the best life I can live. I eat a healthy breakfast every morning. I try to hit the gym at least three to five times a week depending on my workload and schedule. Being a private investigator has its share of ups and downs. I have been able to save a good-sized nest egg, but I have worked far too many hours to build it. I recently started my own agency right out of the comfort of my own home office. I have never been happier with any decision I have made. I have no travel time to get to my office, which allows for more hits of the snooze button.

After breakfast, I settle in at my desk to do some catching up. I check my emails from both my personal and work accounts. I do my best to never mix work with pleasure. It always amazes me how much spam mail makes it to my inboxes. How do these scammers continue to find me? How many of them are there? Do they ever stop?

As a private investigator, I have worked a majority of cases based on one spouse or another looking for information about their partner. Sometimes it is the wife who is so insecure in herself that she is sure her husband is having an affair with his new hot secretary. Sometimes, though, this does turn out to be the case. It is not always that simple. I had a client once who paid me to follow her husband around for a full month at $1,000 a week to prove he was being unfaithful. It turned out that he was working two different jobs just so he could save up enough to pay for the boob job that she had wanted for years while still maintaining the lifestyle that she demanded.

I have also worked quite a few jobs for husbands-to-be who wanted to know everything about the woman they were about to marry before saying "I do" and for husbands who thought their wives were trying to kill them. You can never be too careful these days, especially when you have the kind of money most of my clientele have. Black widows do exist, and they do not all have eight legs.

I guess you could say marital issues are my specialty. Thankfully people continue to get married even with the divorce rate skyrocketing. After everything I have seen and heard spouses do to each other, it is no wonder I have chosen the bachelor life for myself. But who am I to complain? If it was not for them, I would not be the success I am today.

I do occasionally handle different kinds of cases for my clients. I have done a few missing person cases, all of which I am happy to say, turned up in the end, whether they wanted to or not. I do not, however, work on any cases that I would need to carry a gun. I am totally against the use of guns and refuse to own one. I did work on an embezzlement scheme once. It ended up being the man who hired me that was doing the embezzling. He definitely underestimated my abilities and will rot in prison for the rest of his life.

I decide to email all my clients whom I have open cases with to tell them I will be away for the next week. It has been a long time since I took a vacation, so none of them will give me much pushback. There really is not that much going on with the agency right now, so the timing is perfect. The most exciting case I have is a very rich man who recently became engaged to a former porn star. I call it exciting because he has bought me copies of all her videos to watch in case I spot any of her former costars hanging around looking for some action. I already have a folder created on my laptop that will hold all my photos and documents for their divorce, and they have not even made it down the aisle yet. God bless America!

I am not really going on vacation. I just want to be able to devote my time and attention to figuring out what is causing my memory losses. I am, after all, a very good private investigator. If I cannot figure this out for myself I may as well close up shop. How difficult can it be?

I do not know about you, but I would be completely lost without my single-cup coffee maker. Now that was a great invention. Turn it on, let it warm up, pop in a coffee pod, and a minute later, one single-size cup of coffee. No mess and no waste, genius! I can even buy boxes of different flavors if I so choose. Today I am going with Hazelnut Crème, one of my favorites. Pour in a little milk and a couple spoons of sugar, and I am good to go.

I have been trying to remember when I first started experiencing my lapses of time, but when you are dealing with memory losses, it is hard to pinpoint when it began due to it being exactly that, a loss of memory. My best guess would be about three months ago. It may have been going on for much longer, but that is approximately when I started to notice that some things that were happening, just did not make sense. Though most of the more noticeable things would be in the mornings after nights of which I have no recollection at all. Sometimes there is more to it than that. There are times when I will be sitting at my desk, working on a report for a client, and the next thing I know, I will be taking a hot shower only to realize it is hours later. I have no memory of finishing the report or anything that happened in the hours that have passed.

I am starting to feel a sharp pain behind my eyes, which I am quite sure is going to turn into a migraine. Just as I decide to go back to bed, I am suddenly hit with the horribly familiar feeling of dizziness and the unmistakable feeling of nausea taking over my body. Instead of going to bed, I rush from my bedroom to the bathroom. But in the midst of my sprint, my foot catches on something, causing me to lose my balance and fall a few feet before the toilet. I drag myself across the floor, raise myself up just enough to get my head above the toilet bowl, and proceed to vomit. Once I am satisfied there is nothing left to come out of me, I wipe my face with the only thing I can reach from my spot on the floor, Angel Soft, how appropriate.

As I start to recover, I find myself wondering what had caused me to trip in the first place. If there is one thing about me that anyone who knows me will definitely agree on, it is that I am a total neat freak. I have been that way for my entire life.

Everything has its place and should always be in said place. You will never find a dirty dish in my sink.

That is why when I look over my shoulder while still on the bathroom floor and see what it was that had caused me to trip and fall. I know that something is definitely happening with me, not only in my subconscious but in my life. I get myself up off the floor and make my way over to the culprit.

As I bend down to pick it up, I am even more confused than I had been thirty seconds earlier. What in the world is another pair of women's panties doing on my bedroom floor? It seems some women these days like to think if they leave something behind, "*accidentally,*" of course. It gives them a reason to return. Unfortunately for them, I have a no return policy. My collection of women's panties is enough to fill a drawer in my dresser.

I grab a drink of water to wash the taste of vomit out of my mouth then walk back over to my bedroom, shut the shades, grab the pair of panties, crawl back into my bed, slip under the covers, and breathe in the faintest hint of Chanel No. 5, which is lingering once again on my sheets. With my eyes closed, I try to free my mind of any other thoughts. I just focus on the scent I am smelling and the feel of the panties in my hand. It is so quiet I can hear my alarm clock click as the minute changes. I continue to lie there without making a sound or moving an inch for what seems like hours.

CHAPTER

20

MICHAEL

Just when I thought that my life could not get any better, a new gym opened near my place. I had been looking for a new place to work out ever since the last gym I belonged to went out of business. I haven't always been into the "working out and being fit" lifestyle like I am now. I was sort of a nerd and bookworm all throughout my school days. That all changed once I hit my midtwenties and found myself in a nightclub surrounded by shirtless men with bodies I had only seen in magazines or on the internet. I don't think I ever believed they were real. Photoshop can do wonders for those of us who are not so blessed.

These days I spend more time in the gym working my body as hard as I can, than I do on anything else in my life. I am completely dedicated to being in the best physical shape possible. For a man of my age, living the lifestyle I do so enjoy, it is not only my dedication; it is a requirement. After all, how many men in their late twenties can make a living by just standing in front of a camera and watching the lights flash while men and women ogle over them?

As I walked into the gym this morning casually, greeting the hot twink behind the counter who definitely enjoys the attention, I noticed the Now Open sign over the door leading to the new sauna addition. My heart skipped a beat. I have been waiting for it to open ever since the day I joined. It does not matter how many men I have seen naked in my life; there is something about being around other men, especially straight men, naked in a room full of steam that gets me going. Of course, going full commando is not always the option for the straight men, they will usually cover up with a towel, which will sometimes manage to slip down just enough for a glimpse at the prize. The gay men, on the other hand, are usually all in with the full commando option.

I head to the locker room and get ready for my workout, though my mind is elsewhere. It is between busy times. There are not that many other patrons working out (especially any that I would want to see in the sauna), so I stay as focused as I can on my workout. I do my standard thirty-minute cardio routine then hit my chest and back pretty damn hard. When I am at my exhausted point, I decide to grab my belongings from my locker and head for the sauna. I have been trying to keep an eye on the door leading to the new addition during my workout so I have an idea of who I may encounter on my first visit, but I am hoping someone snuck in while I was not watching. If not, my first visit will be a major disappointment.

I open the door as quietly as I can, as to not let anyone who might be in the midst of taking their clothes off know they are not alone. Nothing wrong with sneaking a peek whenever possible. Sadly, there is no one else in the changing room, but I do hear the sound of the jets filling the steam room. Two options: either someone left it running when they left, or someone is in there now. I strip down completely naked, put my clothes and gym bag in one of the lockers, and head to the steam room with my towel hanging over my arm in front of me in case I want to wrap it around my waist once I see whom I will be joining, if anyone at all.

As I open the door, the steam comes out at me full blast. Once it starts to calm down, I am able to see the white of a towel that has been thrown on the floor near the feet of the man that will be stuck in my head forever.

When the temperature in the steam room reaches its limit, the steam jets shut off, and it becomes eerily quiet. With the steam being as heavy as it is, I have not been able to make out much of my mystery man's face or any other part of his body besides his feet when I first opened the door. My imagination has been going wild. I have no idea if he is young or old, fit or fat (what a difference one vowel can make), attractive or butt-ass ugly. Naturally, in my mind, I have chosen relatively young, very fit, and extremely attractive.

As it begins to cool down a bit, the steam thins out, and I can start to get him into focus. The first thing I notice is that he has at some point picked up his towel and put it across his waist, which now adds another question for me to ponder: is he gay or straight? Most gay men I know would have left the damn towel on the floor in hopes of getting some *hot* action. Of course, having covered himself up does not automatically make him straight. He could be overly modest or insecure.

I must say, I am very pleasantly surprised when his features become clearer one at a time. I would estimate his age at some-where between twenty-five and thirty, a little older than I was expecting but definitely not a deal breaker. After all, I am in the same age group. He has a very attractive face and a full head of what looks like dirty-blond hair with bangs just long enough to be covering his eyebrows. I can't make out the color of his eyes though I am imagining them as sky blue, but I do notice his incredible smile when he looks up and notices me looking him over. As for being fit, that is not even a question. It is very obvious from the second I make it down to his chest and abs that he was either born blessed or has spent about the same amount of time in the gym as I have.

I don't want to sound judgmental, but in my experience, you can tell a lot about a man's sexuality by the tone of his voice. As I sit here contemplating how to start a conversation with a stranger in a steam room while being as naked as the day I was born (did I forget to mention my towel accidentally slid onto the floor?), the door opens and in walks exactly what I was hoping to not see: a very fat, wrinkly old man completely nude. The scene has changed dramatically in a matter of seconds. I instantly bend down to grab my towel so I can cover myself, and at the same time my mystery man gets up and walks out of the steam room, leaving me alone with the new arrival, who has of course, chosen to sit directly across from me. I move as quickly to the door as possible, hoping I will not slip on the wet floor and end up butt-ass naked in front of him. As I safely step out of the steam room, I instantly do a quick scan of the changing room, only to find that it is empty.

21

MICHAEL

I check the time and realize I need to get a move on. It is already after 10:00 a.m., and I have to be at work for 11:00 a.m. I am doing a photo shoot for a new men's underwear company that need photos to use on their website. I have done lots of these before. I was a little uncomfortable the first few times, but now it doesn't bother me at all. I am friendly with most of the camera guys, so it is like hanging out in my underwear with friends, no biggie even though I am the only one in nothing but my underwear.

As my Uber driver takes me from the gym to the address that my agent gave me for today's shoot, which looks like an old run-down factory, I cannot stop thinking about my close encounter in the steam room. I do not remember ever seeing him in the gym before. If I had, I am sure I would not have forgotten. Maybe he just joined today? Maybe we have different workout schedules? All I know for sure is, I will be looking for him every time I go to the gym from now on.

I arrive at the location they picked a little earlier than my scheduled 11:00 a.m. time slot thanks to my Uber driver, who did not obey speed limits. Not seeing anyone I recognize, I hang out in the background while they are finishing up with the model doing the shoot before mine. I am not a fan of other models watching my shoots. I always think they will try to copy my poses or my facial expressions, so I give them the same privacy and do not watch their shoots either. Just as I hear someone say "That's a wrap!" I can see my usual cameraman walking toward me. He hands me the pair of white briefs they want me to wear for my shoot, and I head off to get changed.

As I walk out of the restroom wearing nothing but my briefs, they are just finishing switching the background for my shoot. When they are ready for me, I walk over to my spot indicated by the X on the floor, and do what I do best. I let them spray me down with a light coat of oil to make all my amazing muscles glow. Flash after flash, click after click. It is a tough life, but someone has to do it. I have to admit, I do rather like this pair of underwear. I usually do not keep the underwear the companies give me from my photo shoots, but these I will definitely be keeping. I wonder if they will give me any others.

With my shoot done, I head back to the restroom to get dressed. Just as I am about to walk through the door, I spot the cameraman who was doing the shoot before mine. He is standing at a table, talking to someone with his back to me. From what I can tell, it must be the previous model because it looks like they are reviewing photos on an iPad, and I can hear the cameraman telling him how well the shots came out. Once in the restroom, I pull my jeans on over my nice new pair of briefs and throw on my T-shirt. I then slip on my sandals and head out the door.

I do not know why, but for some reason, my curiosity has gotten the best of me. I cannot remember the last time I looked at another model's pictures and wished mine had come out as well as his did. I am very photogenic; the cameras love me! Something is drawing me over to the table with the iPad on it. Both men who were there have walked away, and there is no one else around. I can hear some of the guys in the other room taking down the set they had built for us, but if I cannot see them, they cannot see me. Not that I am doing anything illegal, so who cares if they do see me! It is not like I am going to steal the iPad; I just want to see what they were looking at. I casually make my way over to the table and pick up the iPad. I cannot believe my eyes. Of all the men in the world who can be looking back at me from the iPad screen, it is him, the man from the steam room. His bangs hanging just above his eyes, his incredible sky-blue eyes (which I was not sure he had until now), his beautiful smile, his hard-chiseled chest shining from the oil they sprayed him with. I hold the iPad closer to my face and zoom in on the pair of gray trunks he is modeling, which I have to admit look very sexy on him. I will be a fan of this new underwear company for life.

As I hear the sound of footsteps approaching, I put the iPad back on the desk and turn around, hoping that it will be him behind me, but it is just one of the setup guys heading for the door. I decide to take one more look around in hopes of spotting him, but after looking in the room we did the shoot in and another quick look in the restroom, it seems it is just me and the two cameramen left.

It sounds like they are having a discussion about the newest cameras on the market. I say goodbye and head for the door. My mind is in a fog. I have never been a fan of coincidences; they always tend to freak me out. What are the chances that I would see a man in a steam room at my gym whom I have never seen before and then see him again later the same day doing the same photo shoot I am doing? Can that even be possible? I am positive I have never seen him in any ads before. As a model myself, I do pay attention to other male models, especially the really hot ones. I like to always know who my competition is when it comes to booking photo shoots.

Who is this man, and where did he come from? I am on a mission now. As I stand there on the sidewalk, I take a quick look around in hopes that he is still close by. I have no idea when he actually left the building, so he may still be waiting for a ride. Again, I am out of luck, there is no sign of him. Twice I am within a few feet of him, and twice he manages to vanish before I can approach him. This is a whole new experience for me. I have always been the one people are trying to meet, not the person trying to meet someone else. I am not sure what to make of this, but I do not think I like it. Why am I so intrigued by this man? I have seen tons of very attractive, built, sexy men in my life, but I am feeling very drawn to this one. For some unknown reason, I feel overcome by the need to talk to him.

Still standing there on the corner outside the building, I suddenly have this thought come over me: *Why is he not trying to approach me?* Has he not noticed me too? I could swear I saw a smile on his face in the steam room when he saw me looking him over. Was that my imagination? Was he just being friendly? Did he even see me at the photo shoot? Is he even gay, or is he actually straight?

This is insane. I need answers, and I need them now. I turn around and head back into the building. As I enter the hall, I see the other cameraman packing up his equipment. As I approach the desk, I notice his iPad has already been put away. I walk up to him, and I ask him the only question I can think to ask. "Excuse me, but I was hoping you could tell me the name of the model you were shooting today?"

As he turns around, he looks at me and says, "His name is, Bryant, with a *Y*."

"Bryant, with a *Y*," I repeat to the cameraman to make sure I heard him correctly. I wouldn't want to try stalking someone with the wrong name. He gives me a nod of his head and goes back to packing up his equipment. I am quite sure I have never heard of anyone with that name before in the business. I know I have heard of Bryant College, but a male model, nope.

I take out my cell phone and book an Uber to take me back home. I am still very oily from my photo shoot and cannot wait to take a shower. Once I am in the car, I open the Google app and type in the name Bryant. Once the page opens, very slowly, I might add, I click on the little tab that wants to show me images. This page opens even slower. I sit there with my eyes peeled to my cell phone screen and pray for the images to load quicker. How many men named Bryant can there be? Surprisingly, there are lots of them. From very young to very old, from very rich to very poor, from criminals to lawyers, dating way back in history. It is taking way too long for this to load. I close my browser and put my phone back in my pocket.

When I arrive back home, the first thing I do is plug my phone into the wall charger. It is all the way down to 12 percent after my Google searching. I kick off my sandals, pull my T-shirt off over my head, and work my jeans off. I toss them into the laundry basket and head to the bathroom to take a much-needed shower. As I turn on the shower so it can get hot enough to steam up the bathroom just the way I like it, I check myself out in the mirror. I am still wearing the white briefs from the photo shoot. I want to see just how good I looked in front of the cameras in these briefs before I wash off all the oil. I have to say, my extra time in the gym lately has really paid off. I am jacked and cut. They are going to be very pleased with my photos. I know I would be.

I spend some extra time in the shower making sure I get all the oil off my body, which is not a simple task. When I am finally satisfied that I am oil-free once again, I turn off the shower and dry off. I make sure to hang the towel back on the rod so it can dry out. When I bend down to pick up the briefs so I can throw them in the laundry basket with my jeans and T-shirt, I realize that they have a good amount of oil soaked into them from keeping them on after the shoot. I decide it is probably best to not mix them in with my other clothes, so I leave them there on the floor. I will wash them along with the towel when I do my next load of laundry.

I make my way over to my desk and bring my laptop back to life. With my laptop hooked up to my wireless connection, my image search for my mysterious Bryant is much quicker. Almost instantly I am looking at photo after photo of all different people with the same name mixed in with an occasional photo of the college. I use my mouse to scroll slowly down the page. I make it all the way to the bottom of the page without seeing one single photo of the man from the steam room, the same man that was staring back at me from the iPad. I am completely baffled. How is it possible that a man who is modeling men's underwear does not have one single photo on the internet?

After my failed attempt with the photo search, I decide to click on the All tab, which shows me not only all the photos I was just looking through, but also any news articles containing the word "Bryant." I am now looking at pages and pages of articles, most of which are regarding the college, with photos mixed in here and there. This is becoming very frustrating. How will I know if I am reading an article about the correct Bryant if there are no photos of him to go along with it? I go back to the search bar and add in the words "male model" near his name. "No results found" is what Google tells me.

What am I doing? This is crazy! I have never been the one on this side of stalking. What is it about this man? Why am I so damn intrigued and drawn to him? Why can't I get him out of my head?

22

MICHAEL

There is only one thing I can think of to do at this point. I need to speak to my sister. If anyone can help me find this man who seems to be untraceable, it is my little sister. Although in many ways we are total opposites and have many times been at odds with each other, I know if I reach out to ask her for help, she will not turn me down. I am willing to bet that, unlike me, she is very good at this social stalking business. She will know all the tricks of the trade that I am totally oblivious to and will have no problem tracking him down for me.

My sister and I were always thick as thieves. We were always there for each other, always had each other's backs. Although we were only born minutes apart, I have always been overprotective of her as my little sister. We laughed together, and we cried together. We planned together and we schemed together. I miss those days. We lived through a god-awful experience when we were nine years old. That was when everything changed.

In the years that followed, I decided to better myself. I guess you could say, with my obsession of working out, living a healthy lifestyle, and focusing on my modeling career. She on the other hand, decided to do pretty much nothing. She created her own little world of self-loathing, which through the years drove her to very frequent drinking binges that then led to experimenting with the drug of the day. They say people deal with guilt in different ways. We did just that, from one extreme to another.

Has it really been since the funeral that we have seen each other? Can that be right? Can it really be that many years? As I sit here trying to picture her face and the setting in which I saw her last, it suddenly hits me. It was not at the funeral; it couldn't have been because she did not even show up. I only know she is still out there somewhere because I hear stories, always unpleasant stories, about her every once in a while from random strangers who will tell me how much I look like this woman they had met, usually in a bar, completely wasted and causing some kind of scene. "I think her name was Nicole," they would say.

She is my only sister, but I have no idea how to get in touch with her. I have tried the only number I have ever had for her several times throughout the years, but she either blocked me or changed her number. I have tried finding her on the internet and on every social media outlet there is, but I have always come up with nothing. It is like she does not even exist. There is only one thing I can think of doing. It is a shot in the dark, but I won't know unless I try.

I go to the liquor store close by that Nicole was a frequent customer at, and I am unnerved by the way the cashier looks at me when I walk in and start asking him questions about Nicole. It is like he has seen a ghost. At first, I think he is another one of those gay guys who lose their ability to speak when they are looking at me. I do get recognized quite often lately, usually by gay men or horny housewives who have seen my underwear ads in the stores or online in catalogs. It is a mix or creepy and flattering at the same time. This is a different look he is giving me. It is almost like he is in a trance, and I am not getting a gay vibe from him at all.

I do a quick little snap of my fingers, and it brings him right back to earth. Is he high on something? I ask him what he thinks, and he just looks at me with a completely blank look on his face. He has not heard a word I have said. I ask him if he is okay, and he just nods. He must be high on something. He looks me straight in the face and finally speaks, "Dude, you look really familiar to me, but I don't know why." Here we go again; he is another one of them. I tell him I am a male model whom he has probably seen pictures of in nothing but my underwear. "Don't be gross, dude! Why would I be looking at you in your underwear?" Well, that answers that question. He is definitely not gay.

I am getting nowhere with this guy. "Look, can I start over again? I just want to know if you know a woman named Nicole. She is in her late twenties, tall like me, and has hair the color of mine. I would not be surprised if she has used the word 'fuck' quite often. I know this is the liquor store she would always go to for her bottle of rosé wine." Again, he starts to go blank-faced, he has got to be high. Then just like that, it is him who snaps his fingers. "I know exactly who you are talking about. That is Ms. Nicole, I believe. She comes in here almost every Friday night."

I take the envelope that I had in my back pocket and hand it to him. "What is this for?" he asks me. "Can you please give this to Nicole the next time you see her? I really need to get in touch with her." He looks at the envelope, turns it over and over in his hands, then he says, "Ms. Nicole is a frequent customer and a really big tipper. I will tell her about it when I see her next and leave it up to her if she takes it or not."

Before I turn to leave, I put my hand out to shake his and thank him for his help when I notice he once again has that same look on his face. What is it with this guy? I pull my hand back, say "Thanks for your help," and start heading for the door. This guy needs to lay off the drugs.

He starts talking to himself in a voice just loud enough that I can make out what he is saying. "I know, I know him from somewhere, and it is not from no damn underwear ads. It's his face, especially his eyes that I recognize, not his crotch. I know I have looked into those eyes before."

There is nothing else I can think of to do now except wait and hope she gets my note and reaches out. If she is alive and she gets that note, she will not be able to say no. We pinky-promised when we were little that we would always be there if the other one needed us. I would never break that promise, and I know she would not either.

23

BRYANT

I look over at my alarm clock and instantly do a double take. How can that be? I walk over to the window and open the shade. I cannot believe what I am seeing. Why is it already getting dark outside again? When I lay down in bed to clear my mind and hopefully get my headache to go away, it was a little after 8:00 a.m. It is now 4:45 p.m.! I remember hearing a minute click by on the clock, but now it is over eight hours later. How is that possible?

Focus, Bryant, focus! Even if I did manage to fall asleep, which is very doubtful considering I had only been up a couple of hours, how could I have possibly just slept for another eight hours? This does not make any sense. I walk over to my clock and check to see if maybe something has gone wacky with it. Maybe I accidentally pressed a wrong button and changed the time, but when would I have done that in my sleep? I reach over for my phone and press the home button, and sure enough, it displays the same time as my alarm clock. I try to reach back in my mind to what it was like outside when I lay down, and although I cannot see it clearly, the sun must have been up or at least on its way up, or I would not have shut the shades in the first place. The sun is now on its way down.

I also suddenly realize that my stomach has started to growl. I walk into the kitchen and open the dishwasher. I slide out the bottom shelf, and there sits a bowl from my fruit and granola, a plate from my eggs, a fork, and a knife. I slide it back in and pull out the top shelf. There they are: my glass from my orange juice and my favorite chipped coffee cup. The frying pan I used for my eggs is, of course, already washed and put back in its place. Next, I look over at the place on the counter where I keep my blender, and there it is. If it is really 4:45 p.m., that blender should be taken apart, rinsed off, and sitting in the dishwasher, waiting for its evening washing. That is part of my daily routine. I rinse all my dishes and silverware after I use them, load them all into the dishwasher, and run it every night after dinner. I then unload it before going to bed so everything is clean and ready to go the next morning. I am a creature of habit, I believe they call it. By that blender not being in the dishwasher, I know it should be no later than 10:00 a.m., which is the time I have my morning smoothie every morning.

Nothing is making sense. I am getting more and more confused. I lie down in the early morning after eating my breakfast with the sun rising, and the next thing I know, I have missed my morning smoothie and the sun is going back down. How did eight hours go by in what felt like fifteen, maybe thirty minutes?

I sit there on the edge of the bed with my head in my hands completely at a loss. *Think, Bryant, think,* I am afraid to lie back down in fear of losing more of the day, so I make my way to the bathroom. What better way to clear your mind than to relax under a nice hot shower? For as long as I can remember, anytime I needed to relax or clear my mind, I would turn on the shower as hot as I could without it scalding my skin and just stand there and let it cleanse all my stress and worries away. That is exactly what I need right now. I am starting to freak out, and that is not going to help me figure any of this out.

I walk into the bathroom, hit the light switch to the dim setting, and turn on the shower. I let it run for about a minute to make sure it is at just the right temperature before getting in. While I am standing there waiting, I notice two things that do not make sense to me. The first of which is that for some reason, my towel is wet. Not soaking wet but wet as if it has been used from an earlier shower. The trouble with that scenario is that I take my showers before I go to bed or after I go to the gym. I have not been to the gym today, so why is my towel wet at all? The second thing I notice is that lying on the floor under where the towel is hanging is a pair of men's white briefs. The alarming thing with that is I would NEVER leave a pair of my underwear laying in a pile on the floor, and more importantly, I do not ever wear briefs. I pick them up and throw them in my trash can.

I feel like I am completely losing my mind. In less than twenty-four hours, I have awoken once again with no memory of the night before. Earlier I had found a pair of women's silk panties left on my floor but have no idea how they got there or who they belong to, and I had smelled the scent of a perfume on my sheets that my mother wore all the time, Chanel No. 5. And now, I have found a pair of men's white briefs on my bathroom floor though I do not own a single pair of briefs. I get into the shower, sit down on the floor of it, and put on my thinking cap.

I need to look at this as if it were a client's case that I am being paid to investigate. No slacking off just because it is my life instead of one of my rich clients that is being messed with. I need to clear my head and focus on what I know to be true and see where that takes me. I play it all over in my head again and again until finally one small detail makes its way to center stage.

Let me press rewind one more time in my head, paying very close attention to every single detail, and make sure I am correct. Come on, memory! Please do not fail me now.

I am starting to feel a sharp pain behind my eyes, which I am quite sure is going to turn into a migraine. Just as I decide to go back to bed, I am suddenly hit with the horribly familiar feeling of dizziness and the unmistakable feeling of nausea taking over my body. Instead of going to bed, I rush from my bedroom to the bathroom. But in the midst of my sprint, my foot catches on something, causing me to lose my balance and fall a few feet before the toilet. I drag myself across the floor, raise myself up just enough to get my head above the toilet bowl, and proceed to vomit. Once I am satisfied there is nothing left to come out of me, I wipe my face with the only thing I can reach from my spot on the floor, Angel Soft, how appropriate.

There, right there, *stop!* Okay, now, Bryant, focus, and I mean really focus. As you are sitting there on the floor after just wiping your face clean of any leftover vomit. I need you to dig as deep as you can right now. Is there or is there not a pair of men's white briefs on the floor under where the towel is hanging? Were they there and you just did not notice them with everything that was happening, or damn it, were they not there?

I cannot be 100 percent sure either way at this point, but if I had a gun to my head and was told I had to choose one way or the other, I would go with there not being a pair of men's white briefs on the floor under the towel. I know myself too well. No matter what the scenario may be, if I had seen the briefs on the floor, there is absolutely no way I would have left that bathroom without them in my hand.

This tells me one thing for sure. In the missing eight hours of my day, someone else, I am assuming a man, was in my place, and for some reason, he removed his underwear and left without them. Why would someone have been in my place without my knowledge? How did someone get into my place without me being aware of his presence, considering I have not left all day?

By the time I get out of the shower and dry off, I am completely pruned, but my mind has slowed down enough for me to actually start to relax and hopefully be able to start to figure out what is happening with me. I am starting to feel like I am losing my mind.

24

BRYANT

Get a grip, Bryant! The first thing I need to do is get some food in me. My stomach keeps making funny noises like it is begging me to feed it. I have not had anything to eat since breakfast, and I am pretty sure I threw all of that up. Maybe having some food in my stomach will also help get rid of what remains of my headache, which right now is at least tolerable.

I head to the kitchen and prepare myself a healthy salad consisting of mixed greens, cherry tomatoes, cucumbers, red onions, and some croutons. I then take one of my leftover chicken breasts and slice it up to throw on top. I grab a bottle of spring water from the refrigerator and plop myself on one of the stools I have on the outer side of the kitchen counter. This is where I eat most of my meals. Once I am done eating, I rinse off my plate and silverware and put them in the dishwasher.

I don't know what to do with myself. I somehow missed a good part of my Friday, which is when I usually do most of my weekly chores so I can spend most of the weekend just relaxing, if work allows. I do like to spend at least a good hour at the gym on Fridays and either Saturday or Sunday. I am contemplating going to the gym now that I have some energy back and my head has stopped aching, but I am not a fan of going at this time of day due to it usually being too crowded. I prefer late mornings or early afternoons when it is pretty much empty. Then I notice something strange. For some reason, as I do a little stretch, my chest feels a bit sore and tight. That is how I always hope to feel after I have worked out my chest during my back-and-chest routine, but I have not done that routine in almost a week. I must have hit it extra hard the last time to still be feeling sore this much later. Good for me!

Feeling sore like this makes me wonder if they have finally opened the new addition at the gym with the sauna rooms. I am not really a sauna kind of man. I usually get creeped out by the guys who use it as a way to check out other guys pretty much naked, if not totally, which is not my thing. I typically will not even take a shower at the gym; I wait until I get home. I have heard that sitting in a sauna or a steam room can be very relaxing and can help with muscle soreness. I wonder if that is true.

I walk over to my desk to grab my cell phone so I can give the gym a call to find out if the sauna has opened, but it is not there. I could swear I left it there this morning when I was checking my emails. I move piles of papers in case I had managed to put them on top of it, but still nothing. Interesting indeed. I check all my usual places and find it plugged into the wall charger, fully charged. I have no recollection of plugging it in, but at least it is charged. I dial the number for the gym, and some young guy with a high-pitched voice answers the phone. I know exactly which one he is. He looks me up and down every time he sees me walk in. He does not even try to hide that he is doing it. No shame in his game, I guess. I ask him very nicely if the sauna has opened, and he responds with what sounds like his attempt at a seductive voice and says, "It sure has." I thank him and hang up. I suddenly feel dirty.

I grab my gym bag and throw in a beach-sized towel, which I will be able to cover most of my body with, if need be. I grab my gym bottle and fill it almost to the top with ice before filling it the rest of the way with what is left in my bottle of spring water. I grab a pair of sandals and throw them in the bag as well. That should do it. By the time I have everything ready to go, my Uber is waiting for me outside. I open the door, throw my gym bag in first, then slide in next to it. My driver is one of the friendlier ones I have had lately. He is definitely a talker. As he continues to talk, I am struck by the feeling that I have heard his voice before, but I cannot put a face to it. I try to catch a glimpse of his face. However, I can only see a little of his profile, and he is wearing a baseball cap and dark sunglasses. He can tell from my gym bag and the destination address that I am headed to the new gym in town. He asks me how I like it and what they have to offer, typical small talk, which is fine with me. It is only a ten-minute drive depending on traffic, so why not shoot the shit?

When we are just about a block away from the gym, I am pretty sure he is checking me out pretty intensely in the rearview mirror. I have been getting checked out by women and men for years now. I have been told many times how attractive and sexy I am by random strangers. I have even been approached by a couple of guys claiming to work for modeling agencies whom I could not get away from quick enough. Talk about a bad attempt at a pickup line. At first it bothered me when I started noticing other guys looking at me, but these days I guess I am just used to it.

Then out of nowhere, I hear him say "I got it." I am totally lost; did I zone out and miss what he was saying before that? Then he continues. "I have been trying to figure out where I know you from," he says. "I knew I had seen you before, then it hit me." He must be able to tell by the look on my face that

I am not following him. Why would he know me. I do not know him from Adam, or do I? "You don't remember me?" he asks. As he pulls up to the curb outside the gym, he turns all the way around in his seat and says, "Dude, you must take a lot of Ubers if you do not remember me driving you earlier." What is he talking about? I did not take an Uber earlier. I did not even leave the house today. I very politely say, "Sorry, I don't remember," which is truer than he will ever know, and I get out of the car. I swear I know his voice, and even with the baseball cap and glasses on, he does look familiar to me but not as a previous Uber driver.

That was a little freaky. He must have me mixed up with someone else. They do say everyone has at least one doppelgänger in the world. I open the door to the gym and see the young guy sitting at the front desk. I knew it was him when I called. As he sees me approach, he stands up, leans his elbows on the desk, plants a big smile on his face, and says, "How did you like the sauna?" Luckily, one of his coworkers walks up beside him, and his whole persona instantly changes to that of a much more professional gym employee. He now says, "Enjoy your workout, man." Why was he asking me how I liked the sauna when I am just arriving, not leaving?

I walk through the door to the new addition, which has a Now Open sign above it instead of the Coming Soon sign that has been there for at least a month. As I walk down the hallway, I pass a door that is marked Women Only and make my way to the one that is marked Men Only. I push the door open and can instantly smell the distinctive scent of men's sweat. There are a few benches to sit on and a wall of lockers. Though there is no one else in the changing room, I can hear the sound of hot air being blown around in the steam room. Just my luck, I was hoping it would be empty. I head for the locker closest to the exit and strip down to my trunks. I wrap my towel around my waist and head for the steam room.

Just as I am about to open the door, the timer runs out, and the jets shut off. I turn the timer back to fifteen minutes, hoping I can last that long, but before I can open the door, it opens toward me. A wrinkly, very obese old man bumps right into me. He looks at me and apologizes for bumping into me. He says he didn't see me there due to all the steam rushing out when he opened the door. He then says, "Looks like I am not the only one who enjoys a good steam." I have been told many times that my facial expressions usually say more than my words. This must be one of those times. I am totally confused why he would say that to me when this is my first time in the sauna, and he must have read it on my face because he then says, "Earlier you left just as I was getting here, and now I am leaving just as you are getting here. Enjoy your steam!"

What the hell is he talking about?

25

NICOLE

If I had a dollar for every minute that I spend getting ready to face the world every day, I would be an extremely wealthy person.

Men do not realize how easy they have it. One Friday night I timed how long it took me to get ready to leave my place, from the minute I put my wine glass into the dishwasher to the minute I was ready to walk out the door. I could not believe my eyes when I hit the stop button on my timer app. Did it really just take me forty-five fucking minutes to get ready for a night out at a dive bar? Don't get me wrong, I know I look good, *very* good, I might add, but is it really worth the time it takes? I guess that depends on who you ask.

During my preparation time, I always look forward to hearing Bryant. I was never one for listening to someone just ranting on and on, until one time when I stumbled across Bryant while I was scanning for something uplifting on the radio. I typically ended up with some flashback to the eighties, when music was music and not just someone swearing or bitching about how bad their life is and calling it music. Give me something I can move to, not something to make me want to stick my fingers in my ears and pray it will all be over soon.

Just the sound of Bryant's voice makes the world seem like a better place, even when he is being very judgmental and sometimes just fucking rude. He has this way of making it seem like he is sitting right there next to me while I am getting ready, like he is talking to me and only me. On the days that I do not get to hear him, I get a little bummed out. I miss the way he makes me feel. He does not even know I exist, but he has become a big part of my life. I often wonder if he has the same effect on other people, or is it just me? I am almost thirty, single, and attractive, yet I still have not met a man who can make me feel the way he does with just his voice.

It is Friday night, which means only one thing to me: *party time!* Almost every Friday night for the past few months I have spent at one dive bar or another, mixing with the rest of the lost souls and misfits just trying to find a place to belong. One would think that after investing that many Friday nights, I would have made at least a friend or two that are more than casual acquaintances, but truth be told, I am usually too drunk or high on whatever little pill is in these days to make any real connections. I have come close a few times, but once I stop buying the rounds, they always seem to lose interest.

I like to make my entrance by 11:00 p.m. so I can have one of the best seats in the place with the door in my direct line of sight. You never know who might walk in, and you sure as hell do not want to spot him after some other skanky bitch has already made her move. When I was out last Friday night, I overheard one of the skanks mentioning the grand opening of a new club called Fetish a few cities away from my place. After doing some googling, I found the website for it. *Free* drinks for ladies until midnight. Count me in!

First things first, I need a fucking drink! I do not keep liquor in my place, so I need to head to the liquor store down the street. I check my look in the mirror and notice I look a fright. I throw on a short blonde wig and a pair of dark sunglasses and hope no one will recognize me in this state. It is only a few blocks to the store, so I throw on a pair of sneakers and head out the door.

Even with my wig and sunglasses on, the guy behind the counter knows me the second I walk in. "Hey there, Ms. Nicole, you here for the usual?" I give him a little smirk and reply, "Don't you know it." When I first started coming here, he would not even look at me. I think he was intimidated by my beauty and/or my very strong personality. I do not take shit from anyone. He eventually warmed up to me and started calling me by my name. He has told me several times that I have the most beautiful blue eyes he has ever seen; flattery will always get you a bigger tip. He also knows that I always buy the same exact bottle of rosé. I never buy more than one bottle at a time because I enjoy drinking it too much. If I kept it in my place, I would never be sober. I always make sure I drink the entire bottle in one night and throw the empty bottle out in my neighbors recycle bin the same night. I walk to the cooler, grab my bottle, notice there is only one more in there, and make sure to let him know he needs to stock up while he rings me up. He lets out a little laugh and says, "Don't you worry, Ms. Nicole, it is already ordered."

With bottle in hand, I head out the door. I only make it about ten steps down the sidewalk when I hear him calling after me, "Ms. Nicole, Ms. Nicole, wait up." I stop and turn around to see him waving me back over to him. I guess he does not want to leave the store unattended. I walk back to where he is standing, and he hands me an envelope with my name written on the outside of it. "What is this?" I ask him. He proceeds to tell me that a man came into the store earlier and was asking him if he knew a woman named Nicole. The man gave him a good description of me, the man even knew the name of the wine I would buy if it was me. Once the cashier confirmed that he did know me, the man gave him the envelope and asked him to give it to me the next time he saw me. The cashier said he was pretty sure the man was describing me though he was wrong about the hair color, which made me laugh a bit. I don't think he has ever seen my real hair color. I thank him as I take the envelope, slip it into my purse, turn back around, and start heading toward my place.

26

BRYANT

I have to say, I could definitely become a fan of using this steam room after my workouts, especially when there is no one else in here with me. It does get a bit hot when the jets are going full blast, but I am very used to hot showers, and there is nothing wrong with a good sweat. I can feel my whole body just relaxing from one muscle to another. It is also helping clear my mind of all the weird things that have been happening lately. I am sure there are perfectly good explanations for all of it.

When my fifteen minutes are up, the jets automatically shut down. I play with the idea of going a little longer, but my water bottle is empty, and I can hear some other guys joking around in the hallway heading this way, my time to go. I really should take a shower with all this nasty sweat I am covered in, but I decide to just dry off with my towel the best I can, throw my gym shorts, T-shirt, and sandals back on, and head out. As I am almost out the main door, I hear the young guy behind the counter, again in his seductive voice, say, "Have a good night." I just keep walking.

It is a nice night outside, so I decide to walk home instead of getting another Uber. I know all the side streets around here, which will get me home in roughly twenty minutes at my normal pace. It will give me some time to go over everything in my head that has been happening lately and, hopefully, come up with a plan of action to piece it all together.

I need to go back to the beginning and start there, but when was the beginning? When did I first start to notice I was missing time? When was the first time I can remember smelling things that were not there or finding things in the wrong place or finding things that do not belong to me? That is where I need to start.

Let me try to work backward and see where it gets me. I started my own agency a little over a month ago. One of the main reasons I decided to go out on my own, besides making more money, was because the memory losses had started becoming more frequent, and I was having a hard time explaining them to the other guys at the office. I didn't like having to lie to them, but what else could I do? Tell them I had no idea where I had been for hours at a time? They would have thought I was crazy, so instead I just kept telling them lie after lie until I couldn't do it anymore.

That was also about the time I started finding panties almost every damn Saturday morning and smelling Chanel No. 5 on my sheets. Before that I would find them every once in a while but, sadly, never remember the incredible nights I must have had or the beautiful women they must belong to. It was also around that time when more and more people started paying attention to me and asking where they knew me from. I was becoming popular around the city with no explanation of why. I was turning into a ladies' man and, safe to say, a man's man by no choice of my own.

If I go back a little further, I can remember sometimes when I would go to the gym and that young guy at the counter would say "Twice in one day" with that big-ass smile of his, and I would just pretend I did not hear him. He was either confusing me with someone else, or he was really bad at hitting on guys. I honestly didn't give it a second thought, though I did start to notice some great improvements with my muscle growth. I was becoming solid and cut, which I was not complaining about. There were also a few times over the past one to two months when I would be doing a load of laundry, and just like this morning, I would find pairs of underwear that I could not remember buying. They were always new and always my size, but for the life of me, I swear I never bought them.

Taking all of that into consideration brings me back to right around the time I found out I would be starting sessions with a new therapist and they were stopping all my medications. Is that what started all of this, or had it already started? I am almost home when I remember I need to get some orange juice for my breakfast tomorrow. I have not been grocery shopping ever since I discovered the grocery store near me will deliver them right to my door, talk about convenient.

If memory serves me correctly, there is a variety/liquor store a couple of blocks from my place. I turn the corner onto my street, and there it is. I was right! Luckily, I brought my wallet with me just in case I had to show my membership card at the gym. I enter the store and head to the cooler with milk, juice, and other dairy products. I grab a half gallon of orange juice and head to the counter. The cashier is sitting on a stool, leaning back against the wall almost to the point of tipping over, with his eyes glued to his cell phone, surprise, surprise. I can see he has a pair of earbuds in his ears, which is probably why he didn't even hear me when I walked in. I make a point of putting the orange juice down loudly onto the counter, and he looks up at me with his eyes without moving any other part of his body. "Be with you in a minute," he says. Is he serious? Isn't he getting paid to help me? Just as I am about to walk out without the orange juice, he puts the stool back onto the floor, takes his earbuds out, and says, "Is that all?" as he scans the bar code of the orange juice carton. I hand him my credit card without saying a word. He has officially got on my nerves. I will not be returning to this store anytime soon. He runs my card, puts the orange juice in a bag, gives me my card back, and slides the bag toward me. I grab the bag and head for the door.

"Hey, wait a minute," I can hear him say. Is he talking to me? I didn't see anyone else come in, and there was no one else in here when I came in. As I turn around, he is doing a leapfrog jump over the counter. Did he forget to give me my receipt? Does he think I stole something?

"Sorry, man, I was so into my game I didn't realize it was you. Aren't you going to ask me if she came in?" I have absolutely no idea what or who he is talking about. Why would I ask him about anything or anyone? "Ms. Nicole, man, Ms. Nicole. She came in here not too long after you left. I gave her the envelope." Is this guy on drugs? What the hell is he talking about? I look him straight in the eye and say, "I think you have me mixed up with someone else, I don't know anyone named Nicole, and I do not know anything about an envelope."

"Come on, man, of course you do. You came in here asking me all kinds of questions about Ms. Nicole. You even knew what wine she buys. You gave me an envelope to give her the next time she came in. I am just letting you know she came in, and I gave her your envelope. That is all, man." The next thing I know he is leapfrogging back over the counter. I just stand there completely confused, my head spinning. As he is putting his earbuds back in, I hear him say, "You could at least say thank you!" He tilts the stool back against the wall, and he is just the way he was when I walked in.

I walk out the door and head toward my place. I cannot wait to be home. My body and my mind are both exhausted. What was all that about, and who the hell is Ms. Nicole?

27

NICOLE

From the directions they have listed on Google Maps, it should take me thirty minutes to get from my place to Fetish. I pre-book my Uber for 10:30 p.m. and open the bottle of wine. One should never leave their place on the way to a night out of partying sober, should they? I know I never have. After my second glass of rosé, I check the time on my phone and realize that it is almost one of my favorite times of the day. One of Bryant's time slots is fast approaching. I turn on the radio, which is, of course, already set to the right station, and I start prepping for my forty-five-minute preparation routine, pre-prepping, I like to call it.

One can never be overprepared when it comes to turning an ordinary-looking person into a knockout of a woman ready to walk a runway. I have never been a huge fan of the hair I was born with. What woman would be happy with straight chest-nut-brown hair with a fucking cowlick that will not lie down no matter what hair product she uses? In case you have not heard, blondes have more fun, or they at least get way too drunk or high trying.

I have a vast collection of wigs for just this purpose. I call them my Friday night collection. I have never left my house on a Friday night without one of my fabulous wigs. The majority of my collection is blond of course, but I do have a few black ones and even a red one. Once I have decided on the color and length I am in the mood for, I make my selection and start combing it out. Tonight, I have chosen the red one, which is long enough to go halfway down my back and has some beautiful curly body to it. After I am done with the wig preparation, I look through my makeup case to make sure I have everything I will need for tonight. When you change your hairstyles and colors as often as I do, you need to have the makeup to go along with the look you are going for. So many colors, so many shades, so many choices to make.

Once my third glass of rosé is poured and Bryant has started talking to me, I move on to selecting my wardrobe for this evening. Picking out just the right outfit and heels can make or break a night out on the town. Considering this will be my first time at Fetish, I have no idea what the dress code is. With a name like Fetish, almost anything is possible. Tonight, I will go with something between conservative and slutty, just to play it safe.

I choose one of my semi-low-cut and dare I say skintight black midi dresses, which looks amazing with my red wig. It goes to just below my knees. I am not a fan of my knees; they are bony and bulky. I try to never let them show. For the final touch, I pick out a pair of three-inch black heels. Anything higher could be dangerous, considering drinks will be free until midnight. I have left one too many bars with one shoe on and one shoe off after being so drunk. I had even twisted an ankle getting off my stool and breaking a heel. Nothing says train wreck quite as much as my reflection in the mirror after one of those nights out.

As I finish off my glass of wine and strip down to get in the shower, I hear Bryant saying what sounds like he approves of my selections but that I will once again be coming home alone. How does he do it, make even the most depressing news sound like something positive and comforting? Coming from him, it sounds just like one of those fucking lullabies my mother use to sing to me when I was young.

There is nothing as relaxing as a nice hot shower, especially with the voice of Bryant in the background. Standing under the hot mist, I cannot hear him well enough to make out what he is saying, but just knowing he is, in a way, there with me is all that really matters. Sometimes I will just stand under the showerhead and let it rain down on me without even moving, feeling the hot water bounce off my skin while the steam fills the bathroom and fogs the mirror. It washes away all my cares and worries in the world, at least for the moment.

Once I am completely pruned from being in the shower so long, I get out and towel myself off. I open the bathroom door, and it is back to reality. The fog from the mirror starts to clear, and my Friday night preparation begins. I slip on a pair of my favorite red silk panties and a matching red silk push-up bra with a little extra padding. Trust me, it never hurts to give the men something extra to peek at. I work the black dress I picked out earlier over my head and shimmy it down over my body. I don't remember it being this fucking tight the last time I wore it. I will need to remember that once I am in the club. Any extra bending over, and it may split all the way up.

I have decided to not overdo it with my makeup tonight. Again, I am not sure what to expect from the crowd at a club called Fetish. I do not want to call too much attention to myself. It makes me uncomfortable having people stare at me. Considering I will be a redhead tonight, I will be going with a nice light shade of green for my eyeshadow. I add some mascara to fill in my eyelashes and just enough blush to bring out my cheekbones. The only thing left to add is just the right shade of red lipstick, scarlet should do the trick tonight.

I put on my wig and secure it in place. The last thing I want is to do a Milli Vanilli and have it go flying off my head if anything freaky happens. Not sexual freaky, of course, but freaky on the dance floor. Which, after all the free drinks I plan on having and my three glasses of wine earlier, I plan on owning. I slip on my heels and check the time. My Uber will be here in two minutes. I grab my small black leather purse and head for the door. Just as the Uber app lets me know my driver has arrived, I realize I forgot one final touch. I run back in and apply just a small dab of Chanel No. 5 to both my wrists.

28

NICOLE

I am not one for talking to strangers if I do not have to, but my Uber driver Frank will not shut the fuck up. I always make sure I know my driver's name just in case some weird shit happens. This is going to be the longest thirty minutes of my life. I prefer it when I get the drivers that cannot speak a word of English. I reach into my purse to get my earbuds to block him out, but of course I forgot to bring them. I try to pretend he is Bryant, but his voice is way too deep to pull it off.

He starts telling me how nice I look, and then he asks me if I have a big date tonight. At first, I think of lying and telling him yes, though it really is none of his business. I know he is just trying to be friendly in hopes of getting a good rating and a possible tip, but he is starting to make me feel uncomfortable with the way he keeps looking at me in the rearview mirror. Eyes on the road, not on me, mister! I decide to go with the truth, sort of. I tell him I am heading to a new club for a night out with friends, a little white lie that will not hurt him.

He is quiet for a minute and then he reads out my destination address. "There is no club at that address," he tells me, and he questions if I have it correctly. I do a quick Google search on my phone (what did we ever do without smartphones?) consisting of the words "Fetish" and "club" and click on the link it gives me. I have him read off the address again, and it matches the one on their website. I tell him it is the correct address. He again insists there is no new club at that address. Now he is starting to really piss me off. Is he the Mr. Fucking Know-It-All of the clubs around here? I tell him it is the grand opening tonight so that is probably why he does not know it exist yet. He does not relent, "What is the name of this new club?" he asks. Out of annoyance I decide to not answer him. I sit there as if I did not hear him, but he is not having it. He is definitely one of those men that always has to be right even when he clearly is not. This time in a much louder voice and with a direct look at me in the mirror, he says, "What is the name of this new club?" He is quickly ruining my night. I was calm and relaxed when I stepped into this fucking car, and now my nerves are all fired up. I am paying this man to drive me, not argue with me. I can't believe I forgot my damn earbuds. To prevent him from getting any louder or getting into an accident because he is watching me in the mirror instead of watching the road, I give in and tell him it is called Fetish. In a much lower and subdued voice, he simply says "Never heard of it" and leaves it at that.

It starts to rain just as we turn the corner onto the street Fetish is on. I have to say I am a bit surprised at the neighborhood they chose for a new club. There are not many streetlights, leaving it a bit darker than one would expect when approaching a potential new hot spot. As we pull up to the building, I instantly think, this can't be right. It looks like an old apartment building. I can see that he is thinking the same thing. He keeps looking up and down the street to see if maybe he passed it or if the app that said we had reached our destination is incorrect, but then he notices a small pink neon sign in a window on the second floor of the building that says Fetish. I contemplate asking him to take me back home, but the thought of having to listen to him for another thirty minutes seems like a fate worse than finding out what this new club is all about.

With a bit of an attitude, I say to him, "Seems you were wrong, Frank. There is a new club at this address." Then I get out of the car. When the app opens to tell me that my ride is complete and asks me to rate my driver, it is all I can do to hit two stars instead of only one. Hasn't he ever heard that the customer is always right? They really need to have an option for non-English-speaking drivers on this damn app.

Out on the sidewalk in the rain, I slowly make my way to the only door I can see into the building. I feel like I am approaching a house instead of a nightclub. I do not see anyone else around. It is like an abandoned part of a trashy city. Part of me just wants to go home, but another part is very intrigued by the mystery of it all. What waits for me on the other side of this door? Only one way to find out. I walk up to the door and push it open.

As I make my way through the door, I instantly think, *Where the fuck am I?* This is not like any other nightclub I have ever been to, and trust me, I have been to quite a few. The first thing I notice is the only light on is the one inside a small cutout in the wall with a sign above it that reads Check-In. As I approach the window, a very large older gentleman slides the glass panel open and proceeds to ask me the strangest question, "What's your pleasure?" He does not even bother to make eye contact with me. From what I can make out from where I am standing, he seems to be watching a wall full of monitors with what looks like multiple different-angle views of different rooms.

Once he realizes I am still standing there and have not answered him, he turns his head and looks at me. I can tell by his expression he is instantly attracted to me. He suddenly has all the time in the world for me. I have his full attention. "What is such a beautiful lady as yourself doing in a place like this?" he asks me with one of the biggest shit-ass grins I have ever seen on his face. Does he seriously think he has a chance at getting a piece of this? Wake the fuck up; that is never happening!

As I stand there looking at him without having said a word, the door opens, and two punk-rock-looking twentysomethings walk in. I move away from the window so they can check in. They walk up to the window, hand the guy a twenty-dollar bill and say "Two for floor three." They have obviously been here before. They know what their pleasure is, and they know they can find it on floor 3. I watch them as they walk away from the window. They head down a hallway, and for the first time, I notice doors to an elevator. They press a button, the doors open, and they get in. The doors close, and they are gone, leaving me alone with this creepy-ass pervert of a man. He looks me up and down again and asks me, "So what is your pleasure, beautiful?" This is getting me absolutely nowhere. Time for me to take charge of the situation. I look at him with the most innocent look I can conjure up and simply say, "I am new here. What are my options?" He proceeds to fill me in. I was not prepared for what he tells me, but I do my best to hide the shock I am feeling on the inside.

There is a ten-dollar cover charge. Absolutely no one under the legal drinking age of twenty-one is allowed on the premises; proper ID is required. Though I did notice he did not check the ID's of the two who just went in. There are three floors above where we are now. Each floor has two separate large rooms. The second and third floors also have a men's locker room and a women's locker room, both of which have multiple shower stalls. The larger rooms are separated by the locker rooms. Each large room has what he refers to as its own fetish theme. The themes go from what I would consider a normal everyday nightclub, which is on the first floor, behind the elevator, to a variety of different fetishes. The second floor has a Lesbian Only room on one side and a Gay Men Only room on the other side, both of which are clothing optional. From the way he explains them to me, they are set up like bath houses where anything goes! Condoms are, of course, supplied free of charge. The third floor, which is where the two who just checked in are headed, has a swingers' room on one side, which is open to any and all types of couples and an S-M dungeon theme room on the other side. He assures me they have available every possible whip and chain any dominatrix could possibly want. The last floor has a transsexual room on one side and a crossdressers' room on the other side. I now understand the reasoning for the locker rooms with shower stalls.

As I try to absorb everything he is telling me, all I keep thinking about is how much longer are the drinks free? I check my phone, and see that I have been listening to this pervert talk for almost fifteen minutes, which only leaves me forty-five minutes of free drinks. I hand him a ten-dollar bill and tell him my pleasure is the nearest bar. I need to have a drink in my hand pronto after everything he has just told me.

I make my way down the hall and head behind the elevator to the actual nightclub. At least now I get why they named it Fetish, and I also get why he asked me what my pleasure was. I can hear the music before I am even through the door. It is my kind of jam. Things are looking up. It is pretty dark even in this part of the building, but I am okay with it. I walk up to the bar and order myself a nice glass of rosé. The three glasses I had at my place are starting to wear off, so I have some making up to do. Once I have my glass, I select a seat which faces the door. I need to keep an eye out for any eye candy I may want to venture to another floor with later. I do a full scan of the room and notice that there are only a handful of other losers here, all of whom seem to be together and are already working up a sweat on the dancefloor. I sure hope things start to pick up, or this is going to be a dud of a night. Thank God the drinks are free, because I am just about ready for another.

With my second glass of rosé working its way into my system very nicely, I make my way across the dance floor to the ladies' room. I need to powder my nose and make sure I am still looking as hot as I was before I got stuck standing in the rain. You never know who I may bump into, though in a place like this, I am not exactly sure I want to know. The ladies' room is surprisingly bright and cheery, not at all what I was expecting. It almost seems out of place after hearing what the rest of the building has to offer. I am all alone, which is as I expected, considering I have only seen one woman on the dance floor and one other one behind the bar. I check myself in the mirror, do a little touch-up here and there, do a little lift of my bra, and head for the door.

Just as I reach for the doorknob I stop and look around the room. There are no speakers in here, and there is no one else in here with me. I already did a quick look under the stall doors, yet I could swear I heard someone talking. The voice was very low, so I am not sure what it was I heard. Was it my imagination? Then I remember when I first walked in, the creepy guy at the window was watching a wall of monitors. Is he watching me now? Was that him talking to me through a tiny speaker planted somewhere with one of his tiny-ass spy cameras? Isn't that illegal?

Now I am a mix of pissed off and creeped out. "What the fuck kind of place is this?" I grab the doorknob, ready to head right for the pervert and catch him in the act when it happens again. This time it is just loud enough for me to make out, but it does not make sense. None of it makes any sense at all. How is this happening?

In a voice just loud enough for me to hear, Bryant asks me, "What is your pleasure, Nicole?"

29

NICOLE

I stop in my tracks, close the door, and walk back to the center of the ladies' room. I would know that voice anywhere. It was definitely Bryant, but he has never once used my name before. How can this be happening? I start scanning every inch of the room. I open all the stall doors in case someone, Bryant, was sitting up on the toilet so I could not see his feet when I looked under the doors before, nothing. I even feel inside the toilet paper dispensers, nothing. I look inside the light fixtures, and again nothing. I cannot find any cameras or speakers.

I make my way out of the ladies' room and back to the old pervert sitting behind the glass in his little room with a wall full of monitors. Something on one of them seems to have his full attention, he has not even noticed me approaching. I step closer and tap on the glass. He jolts back in his seat and turns my way. Again, I can tell he likes what he sees as much as what he was watching on his screen. He slides the window open and gives me that same shit-ass grin and says, "Have you decided on a floor? I can send you right up." In as calm of a voice as I can manage at this point, I ask him if he enjoys watching ladies without them knowing. He seems a bit confused by this and proceeds to tell me that there are signs posted in all the rooms, letting people know that they are being monitored for their own safety. I am pretty sure that I have read somewhere that having any kind of cameras in a restroom is illegal, and I let him know it. His shit-ass grin has now changed to that of a puzzled look. He assures me that he has no idea what I am talking about. "Look, lady, we do not have any cameras in the restrooms or in the locker rooms. Those are the only places we do not monitor. Again, we have signs in all the other rooms. Everything is on the up and up here at Fetish." I look at him with what I can only imagine is a very disgusted look on my face and simply say, "Somehow I doubt that."

He starts to slide the window closed, but I put my hand in the way and stop it. I am not done with him yet. "If you were not just watching me in the ladies' room, then how did you know I was in there?" I am assuming at this point that he remembered my name from when he looked at my ID. He removes his hand from the window and places it on his hip while he does the same with his other one. He is clearly losing his patience with me, but I do not give a fuck. I want answers, and I want them now. His tone is completely different with me now as he again proclaims his innocence. "Look, lady, I have no idea what you are talking about. How would I know you were in the ladies' room? I already told you there are no cameras in there." Then an even more puzzled look comes over his face as he says, "Hold up there. What makes you think I was watching you in the first place?" I was waiting for him to ask me that. Time to call his bluff. Let's see how he gets out of this. I look him straight in the eye and let him have it, "If you were not watching me, then how did you know I was in there? If you were not watching me, then how did you know I would hear you when you spoke to me through your hidden speaker?" His face has now gone from a shit-ass grin, to a puzzled look to now a completely shocked look. "Look, lady, I assure you, I was not watching you. And I can also assure you I did not speak to you through a speaker. We do not have any hidden speakers in the ladies' room or anywhere else in the building." This time he grabs the glass window and slams it shut. He is clearly done with me. He sits back down and turns his attention back to his wall of monitors.

How much have I had to drink? Is it possible that I imagined hearing Bryant? I do feel lonely at times and wish I was able to hear him anytime I like, but this doesn't make sense. How could I have heard him in a room that I was completely alone in with no speakers (or so I was told)? The more serious questions that I had almost forgotten about after my confrontation with the old pervert is "How in the world does Bryant know my name?" and "How did he know I would hear him in the ladies' room in a club called Fetish?"

I take my phone out of my purse. It is not even midnight yet, but I open the Uber app and book myself a ride home. I suddenly do not feel comfortable or safe here. I never even made it to a different floor, but honestly, I am not sure what room I would have picked. The app tells me my driver will arrive in three minutes. It is still raining outside, so I stand in the little entryway while I wait. No sense messing up my wig more than I have to. There is a little table against the wall just to the left of the window with the pervert behind it. On the table sits a fishbowl filled with what looks like matchbooks. I reach in and take one out. On the front cover it simply reads "Fetish," and on the back cover it asks, "What is yours?"

My phone dings to let me know my ride has arrived. I put the matchbook in my purse along with my phone and make my way outside. Through the rain I can see the brake lights of the car that is waiting for me. Just my luck, it is fucking Frank again. Could this night get any worse?

I open the door and get in. Frank instantly recognizes me, and before I can even close the damn door, he says, "So how is the new club?" If it was not raining, I would get right back out of the car, but I am up to my nipples in rosé and completely stressed out after what happened, so I sit back, pull the door shut as hard as I can and simply say "Just fucking drive," and he does just that.

By the grace of God, for the next thirty minutes, we ride in silence. I can't help but wonder if he noticed my two-star rating from my previous ride. After what happened in the bathroom of that club, I need silence more than anything. I do not feel even remotely as drunk as I usually end up feeling on my Friday nights out, so the possibility that I imagined hearing Bryant talk directly to me is very slim. I also did not have a chance to score a pick-me-up in the shape of a little white pill, so that is off the table too. Where does that leave me? The pervert must be lying about there not being a speaker in that ladies' room. Even that leaves a question unanswered. If there is one thing I am sure of, it was definitely Bryant's voice I heard. So how in the world did that old pervert get his voice to sound like Bryant's voice?

When we arrive at my address, I tell Frank to have a good night, and he responds in a low, calm voice, "Same to you." This time when my app asks me for my rating, he goes all the way to four stars. My way of saying, "Thank you, Frank, for shutting the fuck up!" As I go to put my phone away, I notice that it is still early, well, early for me, that is. What a waste of a Friday night! I did not get to dance or meet anyone new. Not that it would have led to anything, but I do enjoy getting my flirt on.

CHAPTER

30

NICOLE

I let myself into my place, take off my heels, slip my dress over my head, and pour myself a nice glass of rosé. I turn on my laptop, open Google, and in the search bar, I start typing in the name Bryant, and then I just stop. I sit back in my chair, and for the first time, as I take another drink of wine, I realize I do not even know his last name. I know I have had quite a bit to drink between my three glasses before I left for the club, the two free glasses I had at the club, and now this glass, but what the fuck? How is it that I have never wondered what his last name is before? It is not like he is Madonna or, I guess for the younger people, it would be Adele, whom no one has any idea what their last names are, or at least I don't. I try to think back to any time I have heard his name, and I'll be damned if every single time, it has always been just Bryant. How am I supposed to find out more about him or find a way to contact him with just a first name? I go back to Google, and next to his name, I add "radio" and I hit Enter. I take another drink of wine, finishing this glass, and watch as Google tells me there are no matches found. I fill my glass again and change the words around a bit. I try "radio personality" and "radio host." I try every word I can think of, and they all come back with the same fucking result, "No matches found."

This makes absolutely no sense. How can a radio personality with one of the most amazing, relaxing voices not exist on the internet? I am getting drunker and more irritated by the minute. I pour the rest of the wine into my glass, slip on a bathrobe, make my way outside, throw the empty wine bottle into my neighbor's recycling bin, and head back inside.

Just when I am ready to give up, it dawns on me; I can search for Bryant by using the name of the radio station. He must be there somewhere. They can't have him on their station and not mention him on their website. I walk over to the stereo and turn it on. I select the radio button, and presto, just like that, the radio station is there for me to see, 99.9 FM. I know it must be the right station because I never change it. I go back to the laptop and do a search for the name of the radio station. I am quickly led directly to their website. I look for the section of their staff members and click on it. The page loads with photos of all their staff along with short bios for all of them. I scroll through them, scanning for the name Bryant. Another thought hits me like a slap in the face. Not only do I not know Bryant's last name, but I also have absolutely no idea what the fuck he looks like. Suppose he is that fat old pervert at the club? I do not see anyone with the name Bryant listed as a staff member on their site. I do a second scroll just in case I missed him, but again I do not see the name Bryant anywhere on their page. How can that be? It makes no sense at all.

After taking one last chug of wine to empty the glass, I turn the stereo off, shut the laptop down, wash out my wineglass, hang it back up on its own little hook, shut off the lights, and head to the bathroom. Time to take off this wig and makeup then take a nice hot shower before calling it a night. Once I have finished with all of that, I pick up my panties and bra off the bathroom floor and drop them in the laundry basket. With half of my body under the covers, I realize I never opened the envelope from the cashier at the store.

I get back out of bed and grab my purse. As I open it, I see the matchbook that I took from Fetish. I take it out and throw it in the trash can. I doubt very much I will be going back there anytime soon, if ever. I then take the envelope out of my purse. It is a plain white envelope with just my name, Nicole, on the front of it. I gently open it to prevent ripping what might be inside. There is a small piece of paper folded in half in the envelope. I take out the paper and unfold it. I read what it says and then I read it again. Just when I thought this night couldn't get any worse, I am proven wrong. Four little words is all there is: "I NEED YOU! ~ Michael"

I sit down on the edge of the bed, and tears begin to flow out of me like the gods have opened the river gates. How can four little words affect me like this? I am a strong, independent woman. Nothing should be able to get me into a state like this. I take the letter and the envelope and rip them into tiny pieces and throw them into the trash can with the matchbook. I grab some tissues, wipe my face, and dry my eyes.

This cannot be happening to me, not again. Doesn't he know he is much better off not having me in his life? Yes, at one time we were like two peas in a pod. We had so much fun and shared so many good times together. We looked out for each other, cared for each other, and loved each other the way all brothers and sisters should. He was my protector, and though he never acknowledged it, I was his. What does he want from me? Why does he need me? I still remember that day we were sitting in our tent we had made from the bedsheet, and we pinky swore that we would always be there for each other any time one of us needed the other. He obviously remembers it too.

I slide under the covers, pull them up to my neck, and pray to fall asleep as quickly as possible. Some nights, I could swear, as soon as my head hits the pillow, I am out for the count. Some nights, I will toss and turn for what feels like forever. Tonight is one of those nights. I keep seeing those four words in my mind over and over again. I had purposely blocked his number on my phone so he could not reach me anymore. After what happened the last time we saw each other, I knew it was for the best that we parted ways and had no further contact. He obviously had not agreed with that. He kept calling me and leaving me voice mails throughout the years, which I will admit I did listen to, but I never responded to not even one of them. He was starting to wear me down, so I did the only thing I could think of: I blocked his number so he could not make any further contact. I don't know if he kept trying or if he finally got the message.

After all this time, what could he need me for? What could be so important that he would go through the trouble of tracking me down through the cashier at a liquor store? Is he insane? I think I already know the answer to that one. I believe we all have a little bit of insanity inside us. I don't know what to do. I know deep down that I should not see him. I should just pretend I never got the note and just go on living my life, but can I really break our promise? Could I live with myself knowing he needed me and I was not there for him? What if he is in some kind of trouble? What if he is dying and needs a kidney that only I could give to save his life? Am I willing to take that chance?

I know what I have to do. There is no other choice. I get back out of bed, grab my phone, and open my WhatsApp, which I have a second phone number for. I go to my blocked numbers list, which is mostly men whom I have met on Friday nights, when I was too drunk to even remember what they look like, and find Michael's name. I hit Unblock and just stare at my phone. Am I really going to do this after all these years? Am I going to let him back into my life? I know I will regret this, but…

I keep it as brief as he did. I will make no promises I may have to break. Four little words, just like he sent me. "What do you need?"

31

BRYANT

The next morning, I wake up feeling like a new person. My headache is gone, and fortunately or unfortunately, depending on how you look at it, I remember all the crazy things that happened yesterday. I do notice that I am not feeling as sore after spending some time in the steam room. I will definitely be making return visits.

With all my morning emails read and sent and my cup of coffee hot in hand, I relax into my desk chair. Just as I am closing my email down, I notice I have a notification on my phone, letting me know I have a new text message. I was never big on texting when it first started catching on. I would always say I would never do it, too impersonal for me. These days I would be lost without it. I grab my phone, enter my passcode, and open my texting app. I have one new unread text. It is from a number I do not have saved in my phone, probably a wrong number. Out of curiosity, I open it anyway.

I read it a few times and decide it must definitely be a mistake. Whoever sent it must have entered the phone number incorrectly. All the message says is, "What do you need?"

I examine the phone number closer, but it is not helping me at all. I am not even sure it is a real number; the area code is not familiar to me. I have never received or sent any text messages to this number before. I contemplate responding, but considering I have no idea who sent it in the first place, I decide to just delete it and get on with my day.

Considering I did not get to do any of my weekly chores yesterday, I need to get a move on, or I will regret it later. First things first, I need to get my laundry going. Luckily, I have a washer and dryer in my place, so I do not have to go to a Laundromat. I hated those days, back and forth between washing and drying, making sure to always have enough quarters for the machines. I grab my towels from the bathroom and kitchen and add them to the rest of the dirty clothes in the laundry basket. I start the washing machine for the large load setting, add some detergent, and mix in some fabric softener. I will be honest and say that as a bachelor I do not separate my whites from my colors. That would be racist of me, wouldn't it?

Once the washing machine is about a third of the way full, I start taking the laundry from the laundry basket and loading it into the washer. First, I take out the towels I had just rounded up and drop them in, then as I go to grab more, I stop midmotion. I cannot make sense out of what I am seeing. I stand back up, rub my eyes, and take another look. Still there, nothing has changed. I bend down, reach into the laundry basket, and take out two, no make that three, very confusing pieces of clothing.

The first piece is what looks to me like another brand-new pair of very soft gray trunks. Don't get me wrong. These are definitely my style, but I have not bought any new underwear in months. I look at the tag inside them and see that they are my size, but then I realize that I have never even heard of this brand before. Where did these come from, and why does this keep happening? I drop them into the washing machine. Those I will be keeping.

The other two pieces are the ones that have completely boggled my mind. For the life of me, I have absolutely no idea how a red silk bra and matching panties could possibly be in my laundry basket. I hold the bra with both hands and just stare at it as if I have never seen a bra before in my life. I turn it inside out and upside down like I am waiting for it to explain itself to me on how it got there. I do notice that it is a push-up bra with what looks like extra padding built in. The only possibility is that one of my late-night visitors, whom I unfortunately do not remember, went one step further than just leaving her panties behind. She actually went as far as to drop her bra and panties in my laundry basket. That must be what happened. Nothing else makes any sense at all. I open the trash can and drop these in right along with the oily briefs. What in the world is going on?

I finish loading the rest of my dirty laundry into the washer just as the water is reaching the full line. Luckily, there were no other surprises waiting for me. As the washing machine does its thing, I move onto collecting my smaller trash cans and emptying them into the larger one so I can take it out to the trash bin outside. I start with the one from the bathroom then the one in my home office. Next, I walk into my bedroom to grab the one on the side of my bed. As I lift it up, I notice there are small pieces of paper on the floor that missed the trash can. I put the trash can back down and drop to my knees to start picking up the pieces of paper. They look like they belong to a shredded note. I notice a few of the pieces look like they are a different type of paper, almost like an envelope. I try to remember ripping something up recently, but nothing comes to mind. The private investigator in me takes over, and I start collecting all the pieces from the floor and all the ones that actually made it into the trash can. I sit down on the floor with all the pieces in front of me. I first separate them by the different paper types. One is definitely thicker than the other, which means I am probably looking at an envelope and a letter. Then I start piecing them together. It does not take me long as there are only a few pieces with actual writing on them. If I have them together correctly, which I am pretty sure I do, there is an envelope with the name Nicole written on the front of it, and there is a very short note that reads "I NEED YOU ~ Michael."

I have so many questions going around in my head that I think my head could explode. Who is Nicole? Who is Michael? How did a note from Michael to Nicole end up torn up in my trash can? Is this the same note the guy from the liquor store was talking about last night?

Am I seriously losing my mind one brain cell at a time? I pick up all the pieces off the floor and drop them in the trash can, walk to the kitchen, and empty the small trash can into the larger one, which is almost filled to the top now. As I go to stick my hands in the bag to push the trash down enough so I will be able to tie the bag, I notice something small and black just sitting there, staring me in the face. I take it out to inspect it closer, a matchbook from a place called Fetish. I give up! I honestly do not think I can take one more thing happening that I cannot make any sense out of. Finding a matchbook in my trash can in my bedroom is dumbfounding to me. I have no use for a matchbook, and I have never even heard of, never mind been, to a place called Fetish.

I throw the matchbook back into the bag and tie it up nice and tight. I grab onto the ties and pull it out of the trash can. I slide on my sandals, open the door, and bring the trash bag out to the bin. Just as I am about to walk back into my place. my neighbor opens his door and sticks his head out. "Hey, man, why do you keep putting all your damn wine bottles into my recycling bin instead of your own?" I have never liked my neighbor since the day he moved in. He is always throwing parties that usually end up turning into very loud fights. I have had to call the cops on him a few times in the past. Without even breaking my stride, I reply, "Hey, man, I don't drink," and I walk back inside and close my door. He is getting so drunk at his own parties that he does not even remember putting his own wine bottles in his bin. At least he is not drinking and driving. It seems I am not the only one with a bad memory around here.

My mind needs a break, and I need something in my stomach. I head back to the kitchen. It is time for my morning smoothie, which I somehow missed yesterday. I grab a banana, some mixed berries I have in the freezer, a bottle of spring water, one egg, and a scoop of protein powder. I put it all into the blender, and just like that, a delicious smoothie. I pour it into a large glass, rinse the blender off, and put it in the dishwasher.

I hear the washing machine's buzzer go off, letting me know it is done. I switch the clothes from the washer to the dryer, again appreciating that they are both right here side by side in my place. I throw in a couple of fabric softener sheets, close the door, and start it up. With the dryer going, I head to my home office and turn my laptop back on. It is time to do what I do best, what I actually get paid to do for other people, the whole reason I am taking some time off from the work I love doing. I open Word and start a new document. I make a note of everything I have seen, heard, smelled, tasted, and even felt in the last twenty-four hours. The list is longer than I expected. I read through them and try to put them in the order that makes the most sense, not that any of it makes sense at all.

1. More and more memory losses
2. Wet towel in bathroom before showering

3. Young boy at gym and fat old man in sauna both mentioning my visit to the sauna not being my first
4. Oily white men's briefs left on the bathroom floor
5. New men's trunks in the laundry basket that I did not buy
6. Scent of cooking oil in the air from briefs
7. Scent of Channel No. 5 on sheets
8. Red silk bra and panties in the laundry basket
9. Ripped-up note and envelope in my bedroom trash can
10. Matchbook from a place called Fetish also in my bedroom trash can
11. Cashier from liquor store ranting about a note for Ms. Nicole
12. Noisy neighbor complaining about my wine bottles in his bin

There are definitely more I can think of, but let me start there and see where it gets me. From what I can see, I have two options. I can either head back to the liquor store and talk to that cashier again to see what he can tell me about this Ms. Nicole, or I can find out more about this place called Fetish and see what the connection is. I decide to go with the second option. I doubt the cashier will be back on shift at the liquor store yet, and even if he is, what are the chances he will not be high again?

It is time to start getting some answers. It is time to find out more about Fetish and, hopefully, more about Nicole and maybe even Michael.

CHAPTER

32

NICOLE

That was one of the strangest night's sleeps I have had in a long time. Not only did it take me forever to fall asleep, but then I kept waking up from what seemed like the weirdest dreams ever. It was like I was having someone else's dreams. They did not make any sense to me. I have always been fascinated by dreams and what they could possibly mean. Sometimes I do not remember my dreams at all, and sometimes when I do remember them, I wish I hadn't. I have had several dreams where it seems like I just keep falling and falling. My research into dreams tells me that it is my mind alerting me to my anxieties and insecurities. It is also reminding me that I am not in complete control of my circumstances. Lord, isn't that the fucking truth.

Last night's dreams were totally different. I kept dreaming about a bunch of different things that happened during childhood, but it didn't seem like it was my childhood. When I think back to my childhood, I have some great memories, most of which include Michael. We loved using our sheets to make tents and hide in them like no one else could see or hear us. We would create our own little private world, and few were ever allowed in.

There was this one boy whom we became friends with back when we were around eight or nine years old, I believe. I can't recall his name or how we met him, but he became a regular in our private little world. He was around the same age as we were. He did not have any brothers or sisters or any other friends to play with. We had to start using two sheets tied together to make our tent big enough for the three of us.

One of the games we would play was the three monkeys. Michael would always want to be the hear-no-evil monkey. For some reason, even though he was a boy, he would never want to hear anyone arguing or fighting. He would always stick his fingers in his ears to try to block out the noises. One day we found an old pair of used earplugs, and after a good washing, they became Michael's. The boy would always chime in next to claim the speak-no-evil monkey. He was always telling us stories about getting yelled at by his mother for telling lies and trying to start trouble, which usually ended with him being punished. Though what his parents called being punished had a whole new meaning. That left me with the fucking see-no-evil monkey. Whenever we played, I would take my mother's blindfold she used to sleep at night so I was totally unable to see any evil. I wonder whatever happened to the boy.

I have been putting off looking at my phone for as long as I can. I am nervous to see if Michael has replied. I imagine if he has seen my text from last night, he definitely would have replied right away. My mind again starts wandering, trying to figure out what it is he needs from me. All I know, is it better be something really important. I grab my phone and find my WhatsApp icon, which I have hidden in one of the little folders I created. I had not used it in quite some time, but I am pretty sure if I had a new message, there would be a little notification letting me know. Not seeing one, I open the app anyway just to make sure. I do not have a new message from him, which is very strange. Maybe he had a better night than I did last night, and he is still sleeping it off or nursing a hangover.

All this sudden stress and anxiety about hearing from Michael had taken my mind off Bryant. Dreams of falling seem quite appropriate for a life like mine. I need to try to put Michael out of my thoughts until I hear back from him. I am not about to go chasing him down. I reached back out to him this time. Now it is up to him. Now what to do about Bryant? The internet was a dead end, the radio station was another dead end. What other ways are there for me to find out more about him? Why is it I can hear his voice, but I cannot find him anywhere? It is almost like he does not even exist except in my head. I am starting to drive myself crazy. Maybe a little distraction with Michael would not be such a bad thing after all.

CHAPTER

33

MICHAEL

The waiting is killing me. I need Nicole to reach out to me. Maybe I should have included my cell phone number on the note. She must still have it saved somewhere, right? I have already checked my phone several times this morning just in case I missed the beep letting me know that the text has arrived. My options are very limited for ways to find her. Maybe I should go back to the liquor store and ask the cashier if she has been in yet. He did say she goes in most Friday nights, and last night was Friday.

The weather app tells me it will rain again today. It is that time of year. It rained last night and will probably rain again tomorrow. I really don't mind the rain; it has a way of making things look brighter once it clears away. I get dressed, grab my keys, cell phone, and an umbrella. A short walk to the store in the rain will be refreshing.

I make it to the store in less than ten minutes. My feet are a little squishy in my sneakers from stepping in one too many puddles. I really need to watch where I am walking. As I enter the store, I can see the same cashier is behind the counter. Does this guy live here? I wait patiently as he helps an old woman decide which brand of gum is best to chew with her dentures. Lord, help me. I know the only way to not be that old is to die first, but I am not sure which one is the better road to travel.

Once he has finished helping her, I hold the door open for her to leave, considering she has a bag in one hand and her umbrella in the other. She stops with one leg in the store and one leg on the sidewalk, puts her bag on the ground, and pops her umbrella open. She then picks her bag back up and is on her way without even a smile, a nod, or God forbid, a thank-you. What is this world coming to? What an ungrateful old hag.

"You again?" I can hear the cashier say. He does not seem high today, nor does he sound like he is in a good mood. I walk up to the counter. "I was hoping you would remember me," I say, to which he replies, "Man, I don't know what your deal is, but yes, I remember you. How could I not?" Where is this attitude coming from? Is he still coming down from his high? I need to change the dynamics here; I do not like how this is going. "I was wondering if you could tell me if Nicole has been in yet and if you were able to give her the envelope I left with you?"

Here it comes again, that same blank look on his face as yesterday. Maybe he is high after all. It is like he is here one minute and gone the next. "Man, are you for real? Are you on drugs or something?" What, is he asking me if I am on drugs? Isn't he the one that is high right now? This is getting worse instead of better. Time to grab the bull by the horns. "I'm sorry, I thought you said you remembered me. I assure you I am not on drugs though I am also not judging you for choices you make in your own life either."

His look is now a mix of blankness and just a smidge of pissed off. There is a nice hint of red taking over his face. "Look, man, if you are suggesting I use drugs, you are way off base here, and I do not appreciate the accusation or assumption."

I need to calm him down, or he will not help me with Nicole, and he may be my only way of getting to her. "I did not mean to offend you. I noticed you have sort of a blank look on your face, which I have only seen before on people who are flying higher than high," I say in the calmest voice I can find.

"So you *ass*umed I am high? Do you know what happens when you assume? You make an *ass* out of yourself, which you are doing right now."

Okay, now he is getting me pissed. Did he really just call me an ass? Take a deep breath Michael, calm yourself down, and try again. "Clearly, we are misunderstanding each other. I am sorry if I have offended you." Everyone likes an apology, so that should help.

"Look, man, you must be tripping. First, you come in here yesterday asking me all kinds of questions about Ms. Nicole and ask me to give her an envelope for you. Then you come back in here late last night, and when I tell you that Ms. Nicole had come in a little after you left the first time and that I gave her your envelope, you tell me that I must have you mixed up with someone else, that you do not know anyone named Nicole nor do you know anything about an envelope. Yet, you stand there thinking I am on drugs?"

What the hell is he talking about? I did not come back in here last night. I went straight home from here and passed right out for the rest of the night. Now I am the one with the blank look on my face as I stand there just looking at him. "Hold up, hold up!" I say to him as I try to wrap my brain around what he is saying. How do I word this nicely so I do not piss him off any more than I already have? I cannot afford to make an enemy out of this guy.

Here goes nothing. "Look, I am sorry I thought you might be on drugs. I did not mean to upset you. As I told you, it was only because of the look you had on your face when I started talking to you. You had the same look when I was in here yesterday asking about Nicole. With that said, I can assure you I was only in here once yesterday. I did not come back in here later last night. You must have me confused with someone else." Then I realized that he said he did give Nicole the envelope, and my tone changes to a much softer calm one. "Did you say she came in here last night and you gave her the envelope?"

He comes around from behind the counter and steps into my personal space. I am not comfortable with that at all; I take a step back. "Look, man, I don't know what is going on with you, and I am past the point of caring. If I had a blank look on my face, it was because I was trying to figure out where I knew you from. You seemed to think it was from some gross perverted underwear ads, which I can promise you it was not. It is your face, man. There is something about your eyes, not in a creepy way either. That is why I am sure it was you that came in again last night. When I was giving you back your credit card, I saw your eyes up close. If you don't believe me, check your credit card statement, and you will see the charge from the orange juice you got while you were here. Oh, and yes, Ms. Nicole came in and I gave her the envelope. She put it in her purse and walked away. Now if you could just go, that would be really cool."

I do not know what else to say. I am losing this battle. I thank him for giving Nicole the envelope and walk out the door. I do not even open my umbrella back up; I just walk with the rain pouring down on me. I need to get home and look at my online account for my credit card. I simply do not have any recollection of going back to that store to buy orange juice. I also have no recollection of him already telling me he gave Nicole the envelope. One of us is losing our mind, and I sure hope it is him.

34

BRYANT

After going over the list several more times, the investigator in me decides my best course of action is to follow up on the matchbook from Fetish. I open my laptop and do a search of local companies named Fetish, seems like a good place to start. I see a link for a new club that opened recently a few cities away. I click on the link, and I notice that the logo they use on the website is the same logo that is on the cover of the matchbook. *Bingo!* No wonder they pay me the big bucks. I can see from the website that they are open pretty much 24-7. There is not much other helpful information on the website, so I jot down the address and shut down my laptop.

I look out the window and notice it is still raining. What a waste of a Saturday. "The rain can't hurt you. You are not made of sugar after all," my father would tell me. It was not the rain that I was worried about hurting me. I was planning on going to the gym again today, but I think focusing on what is going on in my life, in my head, needs to take priority. I go to the bathroom, brush my teeth, take a leak, and pop a few aspirin. Please, God, do not let me have another migraine coming on. I have no idea what this place Fetish is like, but I do not intend on staying there long. I just want to go talk to whomever is working and find out if they happen to know anything about this Nicole or Michael. It is too much of a coincidence to me that the matchbook was right there with the ripped-up letter and envelope. I have learned to not believe in coincidences. There has got to be a connection between them, and I need to find out what it is. Bryant is on the case!

My Uber arrives in record time today. I rush from my door to the car without opening my umbrella, which I brought just in case I need it later, so I am a bit wet when I get inside the car. "I thought this address looked familiar," my driver says as he looks back at me while I wipe the rain from my face. Then he asks, "Do you remember me this time?" I must admit, I had not even looked at him at all. I am too focused on drying myself off a bit. I look up at him and realize he is the same driver I had yesterday when I went to the gym. The same driver who told me he had driven me earlier in the day, even though I had not left my place. I swear I know his voice, but for the life of me, I cannot place it. He is wearing his sunglasses again even though it is raining, so I really cannot see much of his face. The puzzling part is that he is saying he recognizes me from driving me in his Uber, but a part of me thinks it is from somewhere else, but where?

"Yeah, sure, you gave me a ride to the gym last night. Sorry I did not catch your name," I respond. I do not bring up that he argued with me about the other ride earlier in the day. Nothing good could come from that.

"No worries. My name is Frank. Are you headed to the gym again today? Not much else to do around here on a rainy day like this."

Talk about freaky, I knew he was going to say his name was Frank before I even finished asking the question. I always try to be friendly to everyone I meet. You never know who could be a future client, but this guy sure does ask a lot of questions. I know he is just being polite and sociable, but I am not in the mood for it today. I just want to get where I am going and do so in peace. It takes everything I have to respond to him, "Not today, Frank, I have other errands to run."

Then out of nowhere he starts to laugh, more to himself than to me. Lord, please give me patience. Please make him stop. Then I hear him say, "You have got to be kidding me. I know exactly where you are going. You are headed to that new club, Fetish." So many questions flood my head. The main two are "Why is it so funny that I am going there?" and "How does he know about this club?" I want to know, but I do not want to ask him. Why did I get this driver again? I must have done something awful in a past life.

"Funny story, man, I drove this bitch there last night, and then about only an hour later I brought her back. Wait a minute, do you know who I am talking about? Man, I am sorry I called her a bitch. I didn't mean it in a bad way. She was not very nice to me just because I didn't know about this Fetish club. I try to know about all the hot spots around so I can make conversation with the ladies, if you know what I mean." All that without even taking one breath. How exactly do you call a lady a bitch in a nice way?

Before he can get going again, I take my chance. "Might I ask why you think I may know this bitch, as you called her?"

In a much calmer tone he says, "Come on, man, I said I was sorry. Yes, she was a little mean and rude to me, but she did give me a four-star rating." That does not answer my question. Then he registers that I had asked him a question, and he responds, "I thought you might know her because I picked her up and dropped her off right next to where I just picked you up." Did I just hear what I think I heard? This same driver picked up a lady from right near me last night, brought her to this place called Fetish, and then brought her back here? Then this morning I find a matchbook from Fetish in my trash can in my bedroom. I think my head is going to explode.

Is this guy for real or is he pulling my chain? I try to match his calmer tone, though inside I am freaking out. "Are you telling me that you picked up a lady last night from right where you just picked me up, you drove her to this club Fetish, and then you brought her back here?"

He can tell I had no idea about what he just told me. It is written all over his face. He is worried he just messed up big time. He really thinks I know who he is talking about. Reading people's faces is something I have picked up through the years, and it comes in very handy. "Look, man, I am really sorry if your lady is stepping out on you like that. I researched that club last night after I brought her back. I got the impression when I picked her up less than an hour after I had dropped her off that something bad had happened while she was in there. She looked like she was spooked or creeped out to me. That is not my kind of place to hang out, not that I am judging your lady for going there."

I can hear his app tell us we have reached our destination. I look out the window of the car, and I am very happy I brought my umbrella. He notices me looking around before getting out of the car. He points to the building across the street from where he parked. "It is that building right there," he says. I look across the street to where he is pointing, but it looks more like a house that several families would live in rather than a club. Then through the rain, I see the familiar Fetish logo lit up in neon pink on a sign in the second-floor window. What am I doing here? I must be out of my mind for sure.

As I go to get out of the car, I suddenly stop, get back in, and ask him one more question. "Can you tell me what this lady you drove here last night looked like by any chance?" I know he is convinced she is my lady and that he just ratted her out to me about stepping out, and I am going to let him keep thinking that.

"I sure can! I have to say, she was pretty smoking hot. She was wearing a *skintight* black dress and about three-inch black heels. She had long red wavy hair about halfway down her back. She has the most beautiful blue eyes I have ever seen. She may have caught me staring at her in the mirror once or twice, but I was so drawn to her eyes I couldn't help myself." Then he stops, almost as if in midsentence or midthought, and he just stares directly at me in silence. It just got very awkward in this car in the matter of a second. What the hell just happened? Was he done talking? Is he waiting for me to say something?

Then he suddenly breaks the awkward silence, "Holy shit, man, I am so sorry. Please forgive me, I didn't know."

Suddenly I feel like I am completely lost. Did I manage to lose time again while in this car? Why is he being so apologetic? I need to end this conversation, or I may never make it into Fetish. "Didn't know what?" I ask him.

His response makes me shiver to the bone. "I didn't know she was your sister, man. I would not have called her a bitch or commented on her looking smoking hot. I only realized it when I just looked at you straight on, close-up like this. Are you twins or something? You both have the same facial features, but it is mainly those blue eyes. They are killer blue eyes, man, just like hers. No mistaking them, man. You are definitely related."

Without saying another word, I open the door and get out of the car as fast as I can. My head is spinning round and round. I cannot even process what he just said. I do not even open my umbrella. I run across the street to the building with the Fetish sign glowing in the window and go inside.

CHAPTER

35

MICHAEL

It is still shitty outside, which leaves me with very limited things I can do to occupy my time and my mind while I wait for Nicole to contact me. I decide I should go to the gym for an intense workout followed by another visit to the new sauna addition. Today I just might venture into the actual sauna instead of the steam room to see which one is better. I think I am going to like the steam room with the wet heat more, as opposed to the sauna with the dry heat, but I won't know until I try it.

As I start grabbing my workout clothes, I suddenly remember how much I liked the briefs from my photo shoot. I looked damn good in those. If there is one way to find out if this Bryant guy is gay, it would be to let him see me in those. You never know, he might be heading to the gym again today as well. Where did I put those damn things? Oh yeah, that's right, I left them on the bathroom floor. I make my way to the bathroom, but I can see before I even walk through the door that they are not on the floor anymore. That is strange. I could swear I left them right there under the towel because I was going to wash them together. I change my direction and now walk over to the laundry basket, but it is empty. Not on the floor and not in the laundry basket. Is my mind playing tricks on me?

I look in my underwear drawer, under the bed, and anywhere else I might have put them, but they are nowhere to be found. Did I end up throwing them out because they had all that oil soaked into them and just don't remember doing it? I check my trash can near my bed, empty. I check the trash cans in my office and the bathroom, empty. There is only one more to check. I walk into the kitchen and check the bigger trash can, but that one is empty too. Okay, I am officially a little freaked out. Is it me who is losing my mind? First the briefs are not where I remember leaving them, then my laundry basket is empty, and now all my trash cans are empty. Did someone come in here and clean up after me? I will be the first to admit I am not this neat of a person. Nicole was always picking up after me, though she never once complained about it. Why hasn't she texted or called me? I know she has the envelope I left for her. What is she playing at? Damn it, Nicole. Don't let me down.

If today is Saturday, and our trash gets picked up on Monday mornings, then the trash bag that was in this trash can should still be outside in the bin, not that I remember bringing it out there. I throw on my gym shorts and my sandals and head outside. As I open the lid of the bin, I can see the bag sitting there. I reach in, take it back out, and bring it into the house. I do not need my nosy neighbor watching me dig through the trash. I sit down on one of the stools at my kitchen counter and proceed to untie the ties of the bag. As I open it up, I am completely in shock at what I see. Now I am really glad I brought the bag back in the house. My neighbor would have had a field day with this.

The first two things that grab my attention make absolutely no sense in the world. I am a very proud gay man. I have never had sex with a woman. I have never even seen a woman naked except for my mother, which is a vision I will never forget. With that said, why is there a red silk bra and matching panties in my trash bag? Is my neighbor putting his trash in my bag? But why would he? I can't make any sense out of it, no matter how hard I try.

The next thing I see is my new pair of briefs that I have been looking for. Yes, they do look like they may be stained by the oil, and yes, they do have a weird oily smell to them now, but I could swear I left them on the bathroom floor. I loved how soft they were when I had them on, and I definitely liked how they fit. Why in the world would I have thrown them in the trash instead of at least giving them a good washing first to see if the stains would have come out?

Just when I thought things couldn't get any stranger, they absolutely do. As I go to put the discarded clothes back into the trash bag, with more questions going around in my head than I can even try to count, I glimpse the front of a black matchbook cover. My eyes are not the best, but I could swear it has the word Fetish on it. I stick my hand deeper into the bag to grab the matchbook and take it out. Sure enough, it says Fetish. I turn it over in my hand and read "What is yours?" on the back side of the cover. What in the world is this doing in my trash? I do not smoke or even burn candles, so I have no need for matches at all. Where did this come from, or even better yet, where or what is Fetish?

If I knew the result of what I was about to do next before I did it, I am not sure I would have done it. Have you ever done something that you have absolutely no idea why you did it, but some part of you made you do it? I think there is a word for when that happens, but it escapes me right now. For some unknown reason I open the matchbook. I guess you could call it curiosity, though what would one expect to find in a matchbook except the obvious, matches. This matchbook, however, held much more than just the twenty little matches. It also held a small little piece of paper, which had somehow made its way into the matchbook and was stuck among the matches. My curiosity is officially piqued. I take the piece of paper out from its hiding place and put it on the counter. I remember the saying "Where there is smoke, there is fire," which makes me instantly think, "Where there is one small piece of paper, there are more." I turn back to the trash bag that is still sitting on the floor, which is luckily not giving off any foul odors, and begin my search. I find almost all the pieces right there on top. I am not sure what is further down in the bag that I might end up sticking my hands into.

Once I am sure I have enough of the pieces of paper to put together, I lay them on the counter and start working on my little jigsaw puzzle. It does not take me long to start majorly freaking out. I start by looking for the pieces that have any writing on them at all. As I put them together, one piece at a time, it is all I can do to not lose my shit as I realize I am reading my own handwriting. The envelope and the note that I wrote to Nicole are staring back at me from my counter.

As I sit there on the stool, majorly freaking out about the letter being in my own trash bag, I notice there is one other piece of paper on the kitchen counter that I had not noticed earlier. I reach across the counter and grab it. When I see what it is, I start feeling sick to my stomach. It is the receipt for the orange juice purchased last night, just as the cashier had told me.

CHAPTER

36

BRYANT

With my head feeling like it may explode at any given moment and the remnants of the storm outside dripping off me, I walk into the main hallway of Fetish. I do not feel like I just walked into a club. The hallway is very dimly lit, which I find very odd, especially considering the time of day. Although it is storming outside, you would still expect there to be some light coming in through the windows, but there does not seem to be any at all.

This is reminding me of the one and only time I walked into the back room of one of those adult bookstores, thinking it was a second room of books and videos. It turned out to be a very seedy room with booths to watch some of the porn movies. I am pretty sure I heard actual people having sex in some of those booths. I could not get out of there quick enough.

I do not see one single person anywhere or hear any music playing. They must be open, or the door would have been locked. I make my way slowly down the hall, and then I notice two things that catch my eye. The first thing I see is a small table in the hallway with a fishbowl on it. In the fishbowl I see a bunch of very familiar matchbooks. I am definitely in the right place. The next thing I see is a small window in the wall with a sign above it that is telling me this is where I need to check in. I walk up to the window and finally see someone else; I am not alone here after all. I also notice that he has a wall full of monitors that he keeps scanning from one to the other. I cannot make out what he is looking at from where I am standing, but he does seem quite interested in whatever it is. He then notices me and slides the glass door open. "What's your pleasure?" he asks me. What kind of question is that to ask a complete stranger? That is when my attention goes from the monitors to him, and I suddenly realize that I know him from somewhere, but I cannot quite place him. I start getting a very strange vibe. Something does not feel right here.

It is then that I decide to do what I should have done with that Uber driver. I reach into my back pocket, take out my wallet, dig out one of my business cards, and put it on the counter in front of him. He looks down at the card, scans it quickly, and then looks up at me. I can see in his face that he recognizes me too. "Hey, I know you," he says in a friendly yet concerned voice. He must be wondering why a private investigator is at his place of work. I do enjoy seeing how uncomfortable some people get just from me showing them my business card. Their minds go on autopilot trying to figure out what they could have done that would concern a private investigator. Good times. He then finishes his thought, "You are the guy from the steam room. The one I saw twice in one day and actually bumped into. Sorry again about that." That's why he looked familiar. He is the fat, wrinkly old man. I am again puzzled why he thinks he saw me twice in one day, but I need to focus on the reason I came here in the first place. "So what brings a PI to Fetish? I can assure you we have all our licenses the city and state require, and there are definitely no illegal dealings going on here."

I contemplate letting him go on ranting about everything he can think of that is not wrong with this place, but I just want to find out what I can, if anything, about Nicole and get the hell out of this place as quick as I can. I look at him with as serious of a face as I can muster up and with as deep and professional a voice as I can pull off and start my line of questioning. "Well, I am here regarding a lady who visited your fine establishment last night. My sources tell me she arrived here at approximately 11:00 p.m. She did not stay here very long for reasons unknown at this time. I have her leaving here under an hour later, just before midnight." I stop there.

Another lesson I have learned through the years is that you never want to give too much information, you want them to give it to you. I just stand there looking at him with my serious look still on my face and wait for him to respond. I am having a tough time reading his face. It could be because of all the wrinkles. He is either trying to remember who came in and left around the times I mentioned, or he already knows who I am asking about and is trying to figure out why I am asking about her. When he replies, it is just the way I was hoping for. "I think I know who you are referring to. It is not that busy here at that time of night, and I have a pretty good memory with faces as you already know, considering I remembered yours yesterday and again today." There he goes again, this is not about me, stay focused! I need to bring him back on track. "Can you tell me what you remember about this lady? What she looked like? What she was wearing? Anything that may help me out?"

His description is almost identical to what Frank told me, from the skintight dress to the long red hair and, of course, the beautiful blue eyes. Once he mentions the blue eyes, I switch my line of sight to the counter so he will not be able to see my eyes. The last thing I need is a repeat of Frank's reaction. Satisfied that the same lady from the Uber who was picked up from right where I was picked up, is in fact the same lady that came in here last night, I continue my questions. Time to see how he reacts to these.

"That sounds like the lady I am asking about. Do you have any idea why she left so soon after arriving? Is it normal for your guests to leave that quickly?" I can now see that even through all the wrinkles, he is in a concerned or worried state. I am just not sure why that is. Maybe he is wondering if something bad happened to her, but is he also wondering if it happened here or somewhere else? I let my questions sit there as his face starts cringing and crunching up. He is not liking those questions at all. What is he afraid of? He is definitely hiding something. Tell Bryant, you know you want to.

In a completely different tone, he tries to explain what happened the best he can. "Like I said, she was smoking hot, but she definitely had some issues going on. She tried to act all innocent at first, which was kind of a turn-on, especially in a club like this. But when she came back later to talk to me, she was like a totally different person. She was acting all paranoid and shit. She kept accusing me of watching her, like she was the only hot lady here last night. I explained to her that we monitor most of the rooms here and that there are notices up in all those rooms letting everyone know they are being monitored. We like to call it monitored, not watched. She then went so far as to accuse me of talking to her through a hidden speaker in the ladies' room. I assured her that there are no hidden speakers anywhere in this club. I could tell she didn't believe me. You are free to take a look for yourself if you want to." Then he pauses and changes his tone once again, "Wait a minute, did she contact you about what happened here last night? Is she accusing me of something? Is that why you are here?" This is exactly why I always try to ask just the right questions without giving too much information. You never know where it will lead you. This guy has no idea what is going on, and he is starting to lose it. I need to reel him back in before he shuts down on me.

In a nonaccusatory voice, I try to calm him down a bit but not completely. This guy gives me the creeps, and I am another guy, never mind a lady here by herself. "It is nothing like that. I am just trying to track her down for a client of mine. She is not in any kind of trouble, and neither are you as far as I know. Is there anything else you can think of before I leave?"

He seems to have calmed down a bit though he still looks a little unnerved. I definitely ruined his Saturday. Then I see one of the most popular looks I have seen on almost every person's face I have interviewed. I call it the light bulb look. It is when they suddenly remember something that they think is very important. Unfortunately, most times it is something that I already know, but I did not share with them. Fingers crossed that is not the case this time.

"This may sound creepy, but I am going to tell you anyway since you are asking. One of the rules here at Fetish is that everyone gets their IDs checked before going in. Due to some of the themes in the upper rooms, it is a requirement, so I never miss one. I may not check them for our repeat customers, but I always do for our newbies. I definitely checked this lady's last night. I do not know if this will help you or not, but her name is Nicole."

Call it premonition if you must, but for some reason I knew he was going to say the name Nicole before he even got the *N* out of his mouth. I leave my card with him and ask him to call me if he thinks of anything else. It is all I can do to not turn around and bolt for the door. Ever the professional, I act as if the name means absolutely nothing to me and walk ever so casually down the hall and out the door. Once I am outside on the sidewalk, luckily it has finally stopped raining, I lean against the building and let my investigative mind go to work. I let all the pieces I have gathered start to fall into place.

For about the last three months, I have been losing blocks of time. Sometimes minutes, sometimes hours, and sometimes days. They have been happening more and more frequently over the past three to six weeks. I have been finding things in my place that I do not remember buying. I have been smelling things that I should not be smelling, especially Chanel No. 5 on my sheets. I have experienced several people telling me I remind them of someone else and telling me they have seen me in places I have never been before. Now add in today's discoveries. Frank, my Uber driver, tells me about a lady whom he picked up and dropped off right where he picked me up from. He then freaks out when he believes that he had just called that same lady, whom he firmly believes is my sister due to similar facial features and identical beautiful blue eyes, a bitch. Next add in that this same lady went to Fetish, had a strange or creepy experience there and left after confronting the fat, wrinkly old man, who now tells me the lady's name is Nicole. Let's not forget that I found a set of red silk panties and bra in my place this morning. Now add the matchbook from Fetish and the note from Michael to Nicole in my bedside trash can to the mix.

If I was just another normal private investigator, letting all these pieces fall into place where they fit best, they would most likely lead me to one conclusion. I would conclude that last night I, for some reason, experienced another one of my memory losses in which I somehow ended up with Nicole in my place. During her stay, she tore up a letter from some guy named Michael and threw it in my trash can along with a matchbook she took from her visit to Fetish. She must have ended up naked in my bed leaving her scent behind on my sheets, along with her bra and panties when she left.

For the most part I can see how that conclusion could work, but I am not just a normal private investigator. I try to work every detail, every clue I possibly can into my conclusions. For me to fully agree with the previously mentioned conclusion, I would be overlooking some very important pieces of the puzzle. I am a damn good private investigator; I do not leave even one piece unturned. Therefore, I must disagree with this conclusion. To finish this puzzle, I need to go back to my list from this morning, for without it, I cannot see the whole picture.

CHAPTER

37

BRYANT

I went over my list so many times, I have it almost completely memorized. I remember everything on it, but I might not have them in the exact order as I wrote them down. I need to focus on the top of the list next to hopefully get the missing pieces. I know where my next stop needs to be. I am not sure I will find all the answers I am looking for, but it is my best shot right now. I order another Uber, and this time I am hoping I get Frank again. I have more questions for him.

Sure enough, here comes his car, pulling up right in front of me. What are the chances of him being the closest driver to me again? As I open the door to get in, he starts in right away before I have even buckled my seatbelt. "I figured you wouldn't be staying long and would need a ride back home, so I hung around the area. It looks like your destination address is actually the same as last night, the new gym that opened." I am having a hard time figuring this guy out. Is he just very friendly, or is he a bit on the crazy side? If the roles were reversed and we had just had the same incident we did during our last ride together, I would have left the area as soon as he stepped out of the car. There is no way I would have stuck around in hopes of giving him another ride. I am going to put him at 75 percent crazy and 25 percent friendly. I can handle his crazy so long as he gets me where I need to go safely and answers some more of my questions while doing so.

I want to keep him talking at least until I get my answers, so I go into friendly mode. "Thank you, Frank. That was awfully thoughtful of you. I was actually hoping I would get you as my driver again. I have a couple more questions I am hoping you can answer for me, if you do not mind." I can see from the look on his face that he is a mix of intrigued, happy, and relieved. Relieved that I am not upset with him for calling who I now know as Nicole, whom he believes is my sister, a bitch.

"Sure, man, ask away," he replies.

Here goes nothing or, fingers crossed, something. "I know you had mentioned when you gave me a ride to the gym last night that you had given me another ride earlier in the day. I am curious if you can tell me more about that? For instance, can you tell me where you picked me up or where you dropped me off? Also, why are you so sure it was me that you had given the ride to? I am sure you are giving rides to many different people in one day, so how or why would you remember me so clearly?"

He does not even hesitate with his answers. It is like he was expecting me to ask them. This guy may be a bit on the crazy side, but he is helping me more than he knows. "Funny you should ask me that. I was thinking about it while you were in there. To be honest, I always try to stay in the same neighborhoods. I do not like to be driving all over the place. I prefer staying close to my place, which is not far from yours or from this gym, so if I am on the clock, I am probably close by. Driving the thirty minutes to this Fetish place is about as far as I would go. I don't remember the address of where I picked you up from, but I do remember you were standing outside what looked like an old factory. I also remember where I dropped you off. It was right where I picked you up again today. As for how I remember you so clearly, you might not like this part, but you asked, and I want to be honest with you. From the minute you got into the car from outside that old factory until the minute you stepped back out, all I could smell was some kind of oily odor. I have a very sensitive sense of smell, and I kept thinking I might have to pull over to vomit with you still in the car." He stops talking and looks at me in the rearview mirror. I am not even sure what he is seeing on my face because I am too busy working through what he is telling me. He must be seeing confusion because that is what I am feeling right now. What the hell is he talking about? I did not leave my place earlier in the day yesterday. I was not near some old factory, and I have never in my life smelled like some kind of oil, especially not to the point of possibly making someone vomit from the smell of it.

Then he starts again, "I am sorry if I offended you. I thought you wanted me to be completely honest so that is why I said all that. After feeling nauseous the whole ride, your face is sort of embedded in my mind. I couldn't wait to drop you off and air out my car. Then when I saw you again last night, I almost just kept driving, but I saw you start walking toward my car, and I didn't want to just leave you there. I was very relieved you had showered."

The next thing I know, we are pulling up outside the gym. "I hope I answered all your questions and was able to be some sort of help. I'm sure I will see you around." I simply say "Thank you, Frank," and get out of the car. As he drives away, I just stand there outside the gym and continue processing what he has told me. One piece at a time. That is the only way to put a puzzle together, one piece at a time.

Whenever I solve a jigsaw puzzle, I always start with the border pieces. Once I have the border done, I then turn all the inside pieces over and start putting all the pieces with the same colors together in different areas. I then put those pieces together like they are their own little puzzles. When I am done with that, I put them inside the border. All that is left at that time are the few pieces that did not seem to go with any of the smaller puzzles. All I need to do is figure out where they go, and then, *voila*, I am done. That is exactly how I am feeling right now as I am about to walk into the gym. All I need to do is figure out how the last pieces fit into the puzzle. I do have a guess, but at this time I am not comfortable saying what it is. I need to speak to one more person first, and this is not going to be fun for me in the least bit.

I open the door and walk into the gym. For the first time, I can honestly say that I am happy to see the young gay guy standing at the front counter. He already spotted me and has his big smile on his face. Normally I would just try to ignore him as much as possible, but today is a different story. He is just the person I need to talk to. I am about to make his Saturday a much better day. As I walk up to the counter, he greets me with his failed attempt at a seductive voice, "Hello there, how may I assist you?" *Not the way you want to*, is all I can think of, but I can't say that. I need his help. Instead I ask him if he can review my previous visits with me. I tell him that I think they over-charged my account. It was the only thing I could come up with on the spot. "I can absolutely help you with that," he says while still keeping that smile plastered on his face, followed by "Do you happen to have your membership card with you today?" I always keep my card in my wallet, though most times they do not even bother to check it when I scan in with it. I could be using anyone's card. I take out my wallet, grab the card, and hand it to him. He makes sure his fingers touch mine as he takes the card. I hope he is not this flirtatious with all the guys who come here, or he will end up being bashed someday. A lot of these guys are on steroids and are definitely not gay-friendly.

He scans my card under the reader, and from what I can make out, a very confused look comes over his face. Again, the wonders of reading people's faces. I ask him if there is a problem, and he responds that he is not quite sure. What the hell does that mean? Either there is a problem or there isn't. Not really any other options. He then asks me what my name is, which is strange because isn't he seeing it right there on his screen in black and white? "My name is Bryant, with a *Y*," I tell him. His face changes a little, but not much. What is going on here? Then he looks me in the face, and in a more professional voice than before, he fills me in on what he is seeing. Just like that, the last few pieces of the puzzle fall right into place.

"I am not sure why this is or how this happened, but when I scan your membership card, I see two different profiles. Both profiles have your photo, but they have two different names. One of them is Bryant as you said, but the other name..."

I cut him off right there. I know exactly what he is going to say before he can even get the first letter off his lips, and I am not sure I want to hear it, but I need to. Right here, right now, I need to know, so I finish the sentence for him, "The other name is Michael." To which he acknowledges that I am correct. I tell him that Michael is my middle name, which somehow caused the mix up. "Oh, that makes sense," he says. Which it definitely does not, because Michael is not my middle name. With the puzzle now complete, it is starting to make perfect sense to me.

I thank him for his help and head back out the door. I will walk home from here. The sun has broken through a little, and I need the fresh air to help me clear my head enough to be able to work through my next move. I know what I need to do; I am just not sure how to go about doing it.

Nicole and Michael, I know exactly who you are.

CHAPTER

38

BRYANT

Twenty minutes later, I am back at my place. My brain is completely exhausted. How did I not see this coming? I cannot believe it took me so long to piece this all together. So much for being one of the best private investigators around. I am very disappointed with myself. There were so many signs along the way that I just kept discounting and excusing away. Why wasn't I paying more attention? I need to slow down my brain so I can concentrate on figuring out a solution. I cannot go on living like this, especially now that I know what is really going on with me.

Could I be wrong? Could there be another logical conclusion that I am not thinking of? I go to my laptop, bring it back to life, and find my list I created earlier. What are the chances that I mixed some of them up, which led me to the wrong conclusion? I read all the items off to myself one by one. Not only did I have them all right, I even had them in the correct order. Which means that my conclusion must be the right one.

Sometimes when my stress and/or anxiety is really bad, like it is right now, I will actually sit down in the bathtub and just let the shower water fall down on me for as long as it takes to calm myself down. Some people drink, some people smoke, some people even take drugs, but I take long, hot showers. I head to the bathroom, turn on the shower, and let the water heat up; then I strip down and climb in. I already know this is going to be one of my long visits, so I work myself down to the tub floor and sit down like an Indian would with my legs crossed under me.

After a while, I notice my fingers are starting to prune, but at the same time, I realize that my mind is starting to relax. I am starting to get control back of my thoughts. The hot shower is working its wonders once again. I have done this so many times in my life that I can pretty accurately estimate how long I have been in here by the conditions of my body. Finger pruning usually happens right around ten minutes. Leg cramping, which is what I am starting to experience now, is usually around fifteen minutes when I sit this way. I have also tried kneeling down, but if I make it to even the pruning stage, I am lucky. The tub floor is too hard to be on my knees that long. They start to hurt and go dead on me right around five minutes.

I need to last a little longer. My mind is almost back to a normal speed, which will allow me to come up with the solution I need. I uncross my legs, back up all the way in the tub, and put my legs straight out in front of me. This will do the trick. I close my eyes again and do my best to think about absolutely nothing. I have actually fallen asleep doing this a few times. I would wake up when I fell over and hit my head against the wall. I am almost there now; I can tell by how light my body feels. Like all the weight in the world has been lifted.

Then just like that, I see it, my best option for a solution. A way to put an end to this. I am a bit shaky as I stand back up from being on the tub floor for so long, but I manage to get up, shut off the shower, and step out. As I go to walk, my legs start to give out, so I sit down on the toilet and let them adjust as I towel off. My skin is a light shade of red from the hotness of the water, but it was worth it. Once I am sure I can walk normally,

I get up and make my way to my home office. It is time to put my plan into action. I unplug my cell phone from the charger and open my texting app. I click on the deleted messages tab, open the text message that I now know was from Nicole, and hit the undelete button, which now moves it back to my received messages. I go back to my received messages and reopen the message, then I hit reply. I need to be smart here. Like I have said so many times before: never give too much information. I keep it as brief as I possibly can while still making sure she understands what I am saying.

"I need your help again. Meet me at my place, Monday morning at 9:00 a.m." Then I hit Send.

39

NICOLE

The rain has finally stopped. I always feel like a caged bird when it rains like this. After spending as much time as I do to get ready every day only to have it ruined by the rain, seems like such a waste, so I typically end up spending rainy days home alone. I do not mind being alone with myself like some people do. Some people need to be around other people, like, all the fucking time. I get more than my fill of meaningless conversations with dull people, which I have no interest in actually listening to, on my nights out. The liquor makes it more tolerable.

I guess you could say I am antisocial, which is the complete opposite of my twin brother Michael. Michael is one of those people who cannot stand to be alone with himself. He simply cannot get enough attention, be it bad or good. If someone is not looking at him or talking about him, he is not happy. It makes no sense to me at all. I just want to be left the fuck alone.

I have been this way for as far back as I can remember. It was Michael who introduced me to the boy and begged me to let him into our private world. I was very hesitant at first. I liked it just being Michael and me. I knew I could trust him and count on him to always be there for me and take care of me if I needed him to. He was a persistent little fuck though. He wouldn't give up. He knew I would give into him eventually like I always did, and so we let the boy in.

It wasn't long after that the boy taught us the three-monkey game. We also played hide-and-seek almost every time we were all together. Sometimes we would play for hours at a time. The boy was not that good at finding us when it was his turn. To be fair, Michael and I knew all the best hiding places. Most of the time, the boy would just give up on finding us and leave without even telling us. How fucking rude. I remember one time Michael was hiding for so long that he ended up wetting his pants. He didn't want to give up his hiding spot just to go take a leak. Boys will be boys. It was not all fun and games all the time though. There were definitely times when Michael and I regretted letting the boy in, and then one day, he was just gone. Whatever happened to that boy?

I was so lost in thought that I almost didn't hear my phone when the notification came in, letting me know I received a new text message. I snap back to the present and grab my phone. Sure enough, I see there is a little number one at the bottom of my WhatsApp. I open the app and see the name Michael at the top of the list of my messages. I hold the phone in my hand and just stare at it. The deciding moment. Do I want to know how he responded to my text? Do I even care?

Then just like that, I can see us both so clearly, Michael and me, sitting like little Indians with our legs crossed under us in the safety of our tent. Our two little pinkies tied together, promising each other that we would always be there for each other anytime one of us needed the other. I click on the message and read what he wrote, "I need your help again. Meet me at my place, Monday morning at 9:00 a.m."

Is he fucking kidding me? What kind of response is that? That tells me nothing. Is this one of his stupid games? I read it again, and it makes even less sense to me now than it did the first time I read it. Why is he assuming I know where his place is? We haven't spoken in so many years. I am already regretting responding to him in the first place, just like I knew I would. What the fuck does he need from me?

I sit there and argue with myself. Part of me wants to just delete the message, block his number again, and forget all about it. The other part of me wants, or rather needs, to know that he is okay.

I go back to his text message and hit the Reply button, then I type "Where might that be?" I hit Send, close the app, plug my phone back into the charger, and start planning for my first time seeing Michael after that awful night. The next move is his. If he wants me to show up at his place on Monday morning, then he needs to send me his address. I am not a mind reader after all.

CHAPTER

40

MICHAEL

I know there has got to be a logical explanation for all of this, but for the life of me, I can't even start to make sense of it. How in the world did my note to Nicole end up in my own trash bag? The cashier at the liquor store was very confident that he had given it to her. How did it go from my hand to the cashier's hand, to Nicole's hand, then into my trash bag? What am I missing here? Damn it, Nicole, how are you doing this?

More than ever I need to speak to Nicole. I need her help finding out more about Bryant, and now I also need her help understanding how this letter ended up in my trash. Is that what she is playing at? Is she purposely making me need her? Is she behind all of this? But why would she do this? What could she possibly have to gain?

I can see that the rain has decided to give us a break at least for now. What a waste of a Saturday. Not that weekends are all that different than weekdays to me. With my job, I work when they need me to, which can be any day of the week. Sometimes I find it hard to even keep track of what day of the week it is. I feel bad for the people that work nine to five, stuck to a desk all day long. That is not the life for me. I enjoy my freedom far too much.

I need to find a way to stop thinking about this note, about Nicole, and even about Bryant for the time being. I contemplate going to the gym, but I know if I go, I will definitely hit up the steam room again, and I do not want to take a chance of seeing Bryant again before Nicole has a chance to find out more about him. I don't want to freak him out by *accidentally* being in the steam room at the same time he is again.

I just realized that it is already getting dark outside. Is it really that late already? It amazes me how fast time flies these days. What time is it anyway? According to the clock on my nightstand, it is already after 7:00 p.m. Did I even eat yet today? I am definitely not feeling like I have. I am feeling pretty low on energy. For some reason, I start craving pizza, which is very strange for me. I can't even remember the last time I had pizza. I am pretty sure I still have the app on my phone for the pizza place near me. Nothing like modern technology. I can order a pizza, pay for the pizza, watch the progress of it being made for me, and know when it is being delivered, all on my phone.

When I grab my phone to order the pizza, I notice I have a new text message, which is strange because I have been listening for my text notification all day in anticipation of Nicole's response. I hit the text message icon to open the app and see I have a new message from a number I do not recognize. Seems she did change her number after all. I tap the new message, and I am a bit confused by what I see. For some reason, this is not the first message she has sent me. It looks like she actually sent me an earlier message in the very early hours of the morning, most likely after a night out getting drunk or high, which reads "What do you need?" It only gets stranger from there. After that initial message from her, I see a message that I sent back to her, "I need your help again. Meet me at my place, Monday morning at 9:00 a.m.," which I swear I did not send. The newest message, which I definitely have not responded to, is her again: "Where might that be?" I am not sure why she would be asking me that. She knows exactly where I live. I have not moved in the last nineteen years.

I do not want to give her any reason for not showing up, even though I had no idea she was coming here. This whole thing is strange, but it is what I wanted and needed to happen anyway. I hit the reply button and type in "Same place as before" and hit Send. I am assuming she will arrive on time; she was always the punctual one. You could always set a clock by her. My mind is all over the place today. I can't even remember if I already took a shower earlier today. I don't think so, but the towel in the bathroom is not dry like it should be, and I do not smell of body odor. I throw on a pair of pajama bottoms and a T-shirt, run a comb through my hair, grab a squirt of hair gel to try to get this damn cowlick to lie down unsuccessfully and brush my teeth. I need to start planning my strategy for how I am going to get Nicole to do what I need her to do once she gets here.

ALL TOGETHER NOW

CHAPTER

41

DR. FRANK

This past week has been an extremely anxious time for me. I have gone over everything that Bryant has shared with me and everything that I have picked up on my own more times than I can count. Sometimes it is helpful to read between the lines during therapy sessions due to some patients not being comfortable enough to tell me all the details of their traumatic experiences. Though I do have to admit that sometimes it has led me to the wrong conclusions. Sometimes there is nothing else to read into. I am not sure one way or the other if that is the case with Bryant. He does seem like he wants to share everything with me, and some of the things he has already shared have been extremely personal and painful to talk about. I think he wants to finally tell his story instead of just having it live in the back of his mind. Sometimes talking about traumatic childhood experiences can be very helpful in coming to terms with what happened, accepting that it did happen, and hopefully moving on from it. Don't get me wrong; it will never leave his subconscious, but maybe, just maybe, he will be able to deal with it well enough to get him off some of his medications.

I can't wait for our appointment to start. I made it just early enough to have the water delivered and get myself situated before Bryant gets here. My hopes are high that we will have another breakthrough today. I do not want to force the session, but I am really hoping we talk about the night his parents died. I know he told me in our very first session that he did not kill his parents, but if it was not him who killed them, then he must know who did. I know it is there somewhere in his deepest memories. I just need him to want to remember so he can tell me, or he may never find that freedom he saw out my office window.

I hope he is not going to be too disappointed that I could not find his friends Mikey and Nicki. I searched every way I know possible to find someone, but they all turned up nothing. I thought maybe having their last name would make it easier, but it did not make much difference. It is like they never existed at all.

It amazes me how slow the hands on a clock can move when you are watching them. I have been sitting here for ten minutes, yet it feels like an hour has passed. Then I hear the door opening, and Bryant makes his way into the room. He walks over to his chair, sits down across from me, and I instantly know that today's session will be one I will never forget. Something is different with him today. From the way he entered the room to the way he is looking at me right now, it is obvious that something is not quite right. My first thought is that for some reason, his other doctor started his medications again without consulting me first, but they would not do that out of professional courtesy. I sit here with so many thoughts going through my head that I am completely unable to decide on my first question. Why is he looking at me like that? This is a completely new experience for us. I have never really been able to read his face, but this one I am seeing here now is almost to the point of indescribable. I am starting to feel very uncomfortable in his presence. What is happening? I need him to talk to me so I can figure this out, but he is not saying a word.

C H A P T E R

42

NICOLE

What the fuck is happening right now? I have been waiting to hear back from Michael about our meeting this morning, but he has been dead silent. Instead, some guy comes to get me to take me to some meeting. When I walk in the room, I see a small table with two chairs. There is a pitcher of water and two glasses on the table. There is a man sitting in one of the chairs at the table. As I go to sit in the empty chair, I realize that the man in the other chair sitting across from me is Frank.

I am so confused by what is happening that I feel like I cannot even speak. Why in the world am I sitting across from Frank, the most irritating Uber driver I have ever met, instead of Michael? Where the fuck is Michael? Frank looks as confused as I am. Neither of us are saying a word, which is making it very awkward and uncomfortable. I want nothing more than to get up out of my chair and walk right back out that door.

I can't take it anymore. The silence is killing me, so I break it. "What the fuck are you doing here, Frank? Shouldn't you be out driving someone somewhere while you ask them all your stupid questions?" He seems surprisingly shocked by that. Then he finally speaks, "What do you mean what am I doing here,

Bryant? I am here for our scheduled session, just like every other Monday morning at 9:00 a.m." Well, that did not help at all, it only added to my confusion. Why would Frank think we have scheduled "sessions" at all, never mind every Monday morning at 9:00 a.m.?

I grab one of the cups and fill it with water. I take a big gulp. Not as good as rosé, but I am very thirsty, so it will do for now. "I am not sure I am following you, Frank. The only times I see you are when you are driving me somewhere, which could be any day at any time. Most days I am not even out of bed at this ungodly hour. The only reason I am up this early today is because I am meeting my brother Michael this morning, which is who I am supposed to be with right now actually."

The look on Frank's face must be a perfect match for the one on my face. My head is spinning so fast it is making me dizzy like when you just step off a merry-go-round. I know some fucked-up shit has been happening lately, but this takes the cake. No matter what situation I come up with, none of them make any kind of sense as to why I am sitting in a room face-to-face with Frank. Wait a minute. Did he just call me Bryant, or did I imagine that? That is not even possible. Is he blind or something? Do I look like a Bryant to you? How does Frank know about Bryant? I need to get the fuck out of this room before I lose my shit on Frank.

43

DR. FRANK

This session has gone from awkward to almost the point of alarming, and we have only been together for five minutes. I knew Bryant looked different today, but it is so much more than that. His whole attitude and mannerisms are different. He has never once called me just Frank. From day one he has always called me Dr. Frank. He even asked me during our first session if it was okay for him to call me Dr. Frank. He has also never used the word "fuck" before in my presence. Let's not forget that for some reason, he seems to think that I am his driver instead of his therapist. Of course, the most alarming difference is that for some reason, he is speaking in a much higher voice, almost like a female impersonator would. I am going to have to be very careful with him today, or I may lose him forever.

"Bryant, I did not realize you have a brother, Michael. You have never mentioned him in any of our other sessions. I also do not remember ever hearing about a brother in all the articles I have read. Is he your real brother, or is he a close friend that you refer to as your brother?" This is not what I was hoping to talk about with him today, but we shall see where it takes us.

I reach over for the empty glass and fill it with water. I take a drink, and as I go to put it down, I notice that Bryant is playing with his glass. He is making a bunch of different connecting water rings. Now I know for sure that something is definitely not right. He would never do that. He is the one who always makes sure to put his glass directly over a previous ring, and after the story he told me explaining why he does it, I would do it too.

He has not said a word or answered my questions about his brother, Michael. I am afraid to push him, especially knowing something is off, but I also do not want to waste the entire session. A little nudge and see how he responds. "Bryant, is there something bothering you today. You do not seem like yourself? Did something bad happen this past week that has upset you? You know you can talk to me about anything. That is what I am here for, to help you." Hopefully, that will get a response from him.

He picks up his water glass and finishes the water that was left in it, then he puts it back down in a completely different place without even looking at the table. I am starting to freak out a little bit on the inside. Then he finally asks me a question that puts the first of many pieces into place. In a completely different tone, he asks, "Why do you keep calling me Bryant?"

44

NICOLE

What I wouldn't give for a bottle of rosé right now. This sober life is not for me. Frank has me so worked up. It is taking all my strength to not reach across this table and grab him by his throat. Why the fuck does he keep calling me Bryant? Does he know about Bryant talking to me at Fetish the other night? Is Frank behind all of this? Was it actually Frank who left that damn note for me at the liquor store? I never asked the cashier what the guy looked like who left it there for me. I cannot make sense out of any of this.

I need to calm myself down before I do something I will regret. I need answers, and the only way I am going to get them is to ask the right questions. Time to play nice and see how Frank responds. "Frank, I know you are the one who likes asking all the questions, but if you could kindly answer mine, it would be greatly appreciated." Just in case he did not hear me the first time, I ask him again, "Why do you keep calling me Bryant?"

I know he heard me both times, but he is just sitting there like a cat got his tongue. Come on, Frank, don't stop talking now. In the next few minutes, my life as I know it will change forever. Frank has finally found his voice, "I am not sure why you are asking me that question. In our first session, you asked me if you could call me Dr. Frank, to which I replied that you could. And then I asked what I should call you, and it was you who said to call you Bryant. Do you not remember having that conversation with me in my office?"

Okay, Frank, what are you playing at here? There are so many things wrong with what he just said. What first session? I have never had a conversation with Frank in no damn office. The only times we have ever spoken have been in his piece-of-shit car. Of course, the most fucked-up thing he said was that I told him to call me Bryant. Why would a lady tell anyone to call her by a man's name? Let's not forget that he wants me to call him Dr. Frank. He definitely is not a damn doctor; he is an Uber driver.

Then he has the nerve to come for me again. "If you do not want me to call you Bryant anymore, what would you like me to call you instead?"

Hold up. Does he really want to play games with me? I am definitely not in the mood to play games, never mind with Frank, of all people. "I have a great idea, Frank, why don't you call me by my name, Nicole or Ms. Nicole if you like that better."

45

DR. FRANK

I am once again completely lost for words. How is it even possible that this man has been locked away in a mental institution for almost twenty years, yet no one has ever diagnosed him correctly? I guess it is possible that he is playing games with me, which I know he loves to do, but as soon as he told me his name is Nicole, it was like when you have been trying to find a piece of a puzzle, but none of them seem to fit until finally you pick up the piece that has been staring you right in the face the whole time, and it is a perfect fit.

I need to make sure this is for real. I do not want to be a pawn in a game he is playing or jumping to any wrong conclusions. Fingers crossed that this does not backfire on me. "Nicole it is. While I have you here, I am hoping you can answer some questions for me. I know you already told me you have a brother, Michael, but can you tell me if the names Bryant, Mikey, or Nicki mean anything to you at all? Do you ever remember hearing those names before at any time in your life?" My palms are actually sweating. I am a mix of anxious, excited, and nervous. His next response has so much riding on it.

He fills his glass with water again and drinks most of it all at once before once again aimlessly placing it back on the table. "Well, Frank, that is quite a list of names you have there. If I did not know any better, I would think you are stalking me. I really do not see how this is any of your business, but I will answer your questions. Yes, I have a twin brother named Michael. I have not seen or spoken to him in about nineteen years. He was supposed to be meeting me here today. He said he needs my help with something, but I guess he is not showing up. As for Mikey and Nicki, I am not sure if they are the same ones you are referring to, but when Michael and I were younger, those were the names we went by. The last name, Bryant, is the one that interests me the most. I noticed you were calling me Bryant earlier even though you can clearly see I am not a man, which is fucked up. If you had asked me about that name a few months ago, I would have said I have never heard it before, but strangely enough, there is a Bryant that I have been trying to track down lately. I have never met him or even seen what he looks like, but I have heard him talking many times. There is not much more I can tell you."

Holy shit! It all makes perfect sense now. If I had known I was dealing with a case of dissociative identity disorder from the start, this would have been much easier. I would not have wasted so much time trying to find missing friends who never really existed except inside his mind. Then a thought suddenly takes over me, does he even know they are not real? Is he strong enough to deal with this if I confront him about it? I know when this all started, he refused to talk to anyone, and the doctors here started medicating him almost immediately. That would explain why Nicole has not spoken to Michael in nineteen years. While Bryant, or whatever his real name is, has been medicated, he has not needed them. That also explains why he told me he just made new friends. Now that his medications are out of his system and he has been talking to me about his child-hood, his "friends" who helped him cope with the horrendous things his parents put him through as a child are back to help him deal with it again as an adult.

I do remember in one of our earlier sessions he had told me that we would need his missing friends to learn the whole story about what happened with his parents. I had no idea how true that was. Now that I know what I am dealing with, I am pretty sure I will hear the entire story no matter how ugly it may be.

CHAPTER

46

MICHAEL

Once again, I find myself completely confused by my current situation. I know I am supposed to be meeting up with Nicole at my place this morning at 9:00 a.m., but instead I am sitting in a small dreary room, at a small old table, in a very uncomfortable chair. Unfortunately, that is not the weirdest part of my morning. I spot a clock on the wall which reads 9:20 a.m., but instead of Nicole sitting across from me, I am pretty sure it is the Uber driver who picked me up from my photo shoot last Friday. Why in the world am I sitting in a room with him?

I don't think I caught his name, and I do not want to be rude, but I need to know what is going on here. "Excuse me, but aren't you the Uber driver I had last Friday?" Hopefully he can shed some light on what we are doing here together. Where are we exactly? I do not recognize this room at all. It could sure use some decor. The look on the man's face tells me he is about as confused as I am. Are we not here together? Are we waiting for someone else? Does he know Nicole?

He lets out a little chuckle, not a laugh by any means. It sounded more like an uncomfortable silence breaker. Then one of the strangest things happens, as if this whole situation is not strange enough already, he reaches his hand across the table for me to shake, and he calmly says, "You must be Michael. My name is Frank." How in the world does this man know my name? There is no way he remembered it from my Uber trip three days ago. No one has a memory that good. Wait a minute, he must have recognized me from one of my underwear ads. Now that is a fan!

Then he comes out with the most peculiar thing I have heard in a long time. "Let me guess. You are supposed to be meeting up with your twin sister, Nicole, whom you have not seen in a very long time. If I am not mistaken, you have not seen her since the days you called her Nicki." Okay, so my excitement over having another fan was very short-lived. This man is not a fan; he is an official stalker. How in the world does he know about my meeting with Nicole this morning and that I have not seen her since she was Nicki to me? This man is creeping me out. I need to call him out before he goes any further.

"Frank, how is it that you knew my name was Michael before I even introduced myself, and how do you know about Nicole?" Answer that, you freak. Being semifamous can definitely have its perks, but at the same time, it can bring out the crazy in some people, causing them to become obsessed. I am pretty sure this one is way on the other side of the spectrum when it comes to his level of crazy. He has definitely done his research on me. He not only knows that Nicole is my twin sister, but he also knows that I have not seen her in years. Not to mention he knows her childhood name, which is crazy enough by itself. How in the world could he have found out about that? I need to get out of this room ASAP.

Then he hits me with one more. "It is not what you might be thinking. I only know all of this because I was just talking to Nicole. She told me about her twin brother, Michael, whom she was meeting with today and that she hasn't seen him in years.

She also confirmed that she called him Mikey and he called her Nicki. You actually just missed her. She left right before you got here."

47

DR. FRANK

This session is going by way too fast. I need time to slow down like it did when I was waiting for Bryant to get here. So much is happening at once that I have not been able to get my thoughts in order quick enough to take notes, and I forgot to turn on my recorder app. There are so many bells ringing in my head at the same time. I wish I could stop the clock while he is still here with me so I can put all the pieces of the puzzle together before anything else is said.

I am pretty sure that I have everything figured out except the most important part, who killed his parents. This is what I have pieced together so far. When Bryant was a boy, he was abused in every way possible by his mom and his dad. The abuse by his dad was so awful that it caused him to split his personality into three. He became himself, Mikey, and Nicki. Each one of them took on a different role, which he refers to as monkeys, with special powers to help him deal with the abuse the best he could. It was not like he could escape it; he was living in the same house as his abusers. Then one night something happens, and both of his parents end up dead. When the police arrive, they find Bryant covered in their blood and holding the knife.

Fast-forward almost twenty years, and I request that all his medications be stopped one month before our first session. He starts remembering bits and pieces of his childhood, and the next thing you know, he starts playing hide-and-seek with Michael and Nicole. I have not figured out if he is aware that Michael and Nicole are actually the grown-up versions of Mikey and Nicki. I also have not figured out if he realizes that they only exist in his mind. I will need to figure out a way to get him to talk about them so I can get a better understanding just how severe his case is.

In the meantime, let me see what Michael can tell me while he is here, if he is still here. "So, Michael, I know you have a sister, Nicole, but can you tell me if you know anyone by the name of Bryant? I asked Nicole about him, and she could only tell me that she has heard him talking but has never actually met or even seen him." Hopefully, he can tell me more, though I am guessing it will not be much more. I need to get him or Nicole to talk to me about when they were younger. Do they even realize that Bryant is the same boy they played three monkeys with? Do they remember anything about the murders, or is it blocked out for them too, considering they all share the same mind?

CHAPTER

48

MICHAEL

This Frank guy is really freaking me out. How does he know so much about me? I am pretty sure no matter how much stalking he may have done, there is no way he should be able to know some of things he does. If Nicole was already here, why would she have talked to Frank and then left without keeping our meeting we had planned? Something is fishy here, and I need to know what it is.

"Excuse me, Frank, but did you just ask me if I know someone named Bryant?" I know for a fact that I have not told anyone about Bryant. I was going to talk to Nicole about him this morning, but that didn't happen, so what made Frank ask about him? Frank has this sort of smirk on his face, as if he is saying "I've got you now," like he knows everything there is to know about me even though we just met. Then he feels the need to clarify the spelling for me, "Yes, Bryant with a *Y*, just like the college. Have you heard that name anywhere recently like Nicole has?" There he goes again, bringing up Nicole's name like he knows everything about her too. What is it with this guy?

I am guessing the quickest way for me to get away from him is to answer all his dumb questions, so let's get it over with. "To be completely honest with you, Frank, I have recently encountered someone named Bryant also, but in pretty opposite circumstances than Nicole. You said that Nicole told you she has only heard him talking. For me, I have seen him twice, but have not been able to get close enough to him to talk to him. It is like he is there one minute and gone the next. I have even tried finding him on the internet but have not had any luck." No need for me to go into details about the steam room or the photo shoot. He does not need to know that I am infatuated with Bryant. Some things are better left unsaid.

He is not done with me yet. "Michael, I am going to ask you something that may sound very strange to you, but please think really hard before you answer. Can you try to think back to when you were around nine years old? Do you have any memories of you and Nicole playing a game called three monkeys with another boy around your same age? Can you remember what that boy's name was?"

Okay, Frank has me completely freaked out. How in the world does he know about the three-monkey game? That is a game I will never forget no matter how long I live. We played that the very last night I was with Nicole all those years ago. Please don't make me relive that night again. Once was more than enough. "The three-monkey game was a game that Nicole and I played with a boy named Ryan. I believe his full name was Ryan Hughes. The three of us were pretty much inseparable for about six months. I met him first and then introduced him to Nicole because we desperately needed a third monkey. The last time I saw Ryan was the day of his parents' funeral. Nicole did not show up for the funeral. After what happened that night, she thought it was best that we stayed away from each other, which I found very hard to do. I hadn't heard from her since the night his parents died, until this past weekend." Frank is making me remember a lot of painful memories that I had blocked out for so long. I need for this to end now.

49

DR. FRANK

I knew this was going to be a session I would never forget, but this is even more than I was hoping for. Not only was I able to properly diagnose his condition as dissociative identity disorder, I have also been able to meet two of his other personalities. I am pretty sure there are only two of them as he has never mentioned any other names. Then again, there may be more that he is not even aware of. I really wish I had known ahead of time about his different personalities so I could have freshened up on the disorder before our session. I have worked with a couple of other patients with the same disorder, but I have found that they are all very different individual cases. Some patients are fully aware of their other personalities and some have absolutely no idea about them. At this point I am going with the belief that Bryant has no idea that his "friends" whom he believes he is playing hide-and-seek with only exist in his mind.

I do recall from my other cases that depending on the severity of the disorder was related directly with my ability to be able to get the other personalities to come out and talk to me. Sometimes they would not come forward at all, and sometimes all I would have to do is ask to speak to them by their name.

Some of them love attention, while some of them hate it. Some of them are male, and some are female. Some are straight and some are gay. Some are quiet and shy, while others can be very loud and very mean.

In Bryant's case it seems like he has one male, which he calls Mikey/Michael, who I am pretty sure is gay and loves attention, and one female, whom he calls Nicki/Nicole, who is the loud and mean one. I have not figured out what it takes to make them show up or leave. When he walked into the room this morning, he was already Nicole, but then he switched to Michael without me even realizing he had. It was like what he told me about Bryant earlier. He is here one minute and gone the next. If that is how they always are, it will be difficult holding a conversation or asking questions.

I am fairly confident that between the three of them, I can learn the whole story about his parents' deaths. From what Michael just told me, Mikey and Nicki were there with him the night of the deaths, and whatever happened was so horrific that Nicki vanished before the funeral; he hadn't heard from her since. What that tells me is that with his parents dead, the abuse stopped instantaneously as would the need for his "friends." I do find a little comfort knowing that he kept Mikey around for the funeral. Having a friend there with him, even if only in his mind, was much better for him than being there alone.

I do have some more questions that I need to ask Bryant before I try to get the details of the last time they all played the three monkeys together from Nicole and Michael. I am just not sure how I go about getting him to show up. I check the clock and see that we only have twenty-two minutes left of today's session, which means Bryant needs to show up soon. I reach across the table and refill my glass of water. I take a drink, and I notice that as I go to put it down, his full attention is on my hand. I make sure to put it right back on the ring of water. I look over at him and notice just the hint of a smile.

Bryant is back.

CHAPTER

50

BRYANT

I am so excited for my session with Dr. Frank today. So much has happened since our last session. I have a funny feeling that he may know some of it already. This past weekend I took an Uber a few times, and I could swear that my driver was Dr. Frank. If it was not him, then he has a twin brother. The driver said his name was Frank, but he acted like he did not know me at all. He was wearing a baseball cap and dark sunglasses, and he was dressed much more casually than he does during our sessions. Maybe he was just embarrassed of having one of his patients as one of his passengers. I will ask him about that too.

Oh crap, I must have overslept again. I was supposed to be with Dr. Frank at 9:00 a.m., and it is already 9:35 a.m. He is going to be so mad at me. Hopefully I can sneak in while he is drinking his water, and he won't even notice how late I am. I am still hoping we can be friends once we are finished with our sessions. I sit down as quietly as I can while he is busy with his water and notice he made sure to put his glass right over the ring that is already on the table. Still impressing me, Dr. Frank.

"Good morning, Dr. Frank! I am sorry for running late this morning. I hope you have not been waiting too long. I have some great news to share with you. I took your advice and found ways to tease or tempt Michael and Nicole into coming out of their hiding places. I am pretty sure you will be able to meet them both today! I am so excited for you to finally meet them. You won't believe this, but Michael and Nicole are actually my childhood friends that I told you about a few times, Mikey and Nicki. I couldn't believe it myself when I figured it out. I knew something felt familiar about them but had not even imagined they could be the same set of twins after all these years."

Dr. Frank is just looking at me as if this is yesterday's news. I thought he would be surprised if not even shocked by my news. I feel like a kid whose balloon has just lost all its air. Isn't he happy for me, or is his behavior because he is upset that I have my friends back and he is worried I won't want to be his friend anymore? I need to set his mind at ease. But before I can assure him of our friendship, he fills me in on his morning. "Bryant, I have some news to share with you too. Nicole and Michael were both here earlier this morning, right before you showed up. I had a chance to speak with them both for a bit. They both had some interesting things to say. I do have some questions for you, if you don't mind. My first one is, I am wondering if it would be okay for me to start calling you by your real name, Ryan, Ryan Hughes."

I have to say, Dr. Frank, I did not see that one coming.

51

DR. FRANK

It is a good thing I have had some experience dealing with cases like Bryant's, or I would be completely freaking out during this session. In the matter of forty-five minutes, I have had conversations with three different people though I am alone in a room with only one. I need to figure out what triggers them to switch to make the rest of this session easier for me to manage, but I honestly have no clue at all. I knew Bryant had shown up because of the way he smiled when he realized what I was doing with my water glass, but what brought Michael out for me to talk to? I wonder if it was just me asking about them. When I was talking to Nicole, I asked about her brother, Michael, but I also asked her about Bryant. When I was talking to Michael, I asked about Bryant again. There has to be some logic to it, doesn't there? While I have him here with me, I need to get as many answers from him as I can in case he switches out on me.

I noticed he has not answered my question about calling him Ryan. I better not have freaked him out too much. Another small nudge, "I hope it does not bother you that I know your real name. I asked Michael if he happened to know what it is, and he told me it was Ryan Hughes. I remembered you told me that Mikey and Nicki had the same last name as you, which is Hughes, so I knew he had the last name correct. Then I also noticed that if I took away the *B* and the *T* from Bryant, I would be left with Ryan. That was quite smart of you to come up with that." I can tell he wants to say something, but he seems unsure of himself for some reason. I guess if I had two other people living in my head, I would be somewhat unsure of myself too. Then he makes eye contact with me, and he does not disappoint. "Dr. Frank, I am sorry I did not tell you my real name when we first met, but it is very hard for me to trust people, especially when I first meet them. Yes, my real name is Ryan Hughes, and yes, you can call me Ryan. I really wish Michael and Nicole would have waited around until I got here."

He really has no clue that they only exist in his mind. I think for the time being I am going to go along with that. If I try to get him to realize the truth too soon, the other personalities may vanish, and I will never hear the rest of the story, which I want more than anything. I just need him to stick around a little bit longer with me. "Ryan, would you mind if I ask you a couple more questions? When I spoke to Michael and Nicole earlier, they both mentioned that they had me as their Uber driver this past weekend. I am curious if you had the same experience?" I am pretty sure I know what this is about, but I am looking for some confirmation. It is typical for some patients to involve their therapists in their "private worlds" as a sense of security. They have usually learned to trust us by then, so we are invited in to help keep them safe. The thing is, when they bring us in, we are not their therapist, because in their private world they do not need a therapist. It seems in this case, I am an Uber driver. I would be very surprised if Bryant, I mean Ryan, says he did not see me this weekend. Then the confirmation comes, "As a matter of fact, Dr. Frank, I was going to ask you about that. I think I did see you a few times this past weekend as my

Uber driver, but you did not seem to know me. I figured you were either embarrassed of me knowing you are a therapist and an Uber driver, or you were embarrassed you knew me." Just as I figured, he brought me into his private world with him. At least now I know he really trusts me, which makes me feel good.

Now for one of the tougher parts. I need to ask him about that horrific night again and see how far we get. "Ryan, one of the other things that Michael talked about with me was the night that your parents died. He told me that Mikey and Nicki were there with you that night and that he hadn't heard from Nicki at all since then until this past weekend. I know you told me in one of our earlier sessions that you would need their help to remember the whole story of what happened that night. Which one of them do you think would be able to tell me the missing pieces?" He may not even be able to tell me who knows what, but I am hoping that whichever one can help me/ us will come through and talk to me again. Fingers crossed that it works that easily.

CHAPTER

52

BRYANT/RYAN

My throat is so dry I feel like I have not had anything to drink in days. Luckily there is some water left in the pitcher. It looks like most of the ice has melted, but it will have to do. I fill my glass all the way to the top and drink most of it in one big gulp. I refill the glass again to the top, but as I go to place it back down on the table, I notice there are a bunch of water rings instead of just one. How did this happen? Who in the world would do something like this? How am I supposed to know where to put my glass down to prevent getting punished? Then it happens, just like that, I am nine years old again and living in fear. I cannot take my eyes off the rings of water on the table. I start to sweat and shake. Then I look up from the table and see this man sitting across from me whom I have never seen before, and I instantly wet myself. I know what is coming, and I don't want it to happen. Not again, please not again. I get up out of my chair, carry it over to the corner of the room, and sit down facing the corner. Please, God, not again.

I can hear the man getting up out of his chair. He is coming closer to me. This cannot be happening. Please make it stop. Don't let him hurt me. The man is standing right behind me, and I start praying that I will not hear the sound of him unzipping his pants. Please don't hurt me. Instead he puts his hand gently on my shoulder and asks, "Ryan, are you okay? Why are you sitting in the corner like this?" I do not recognize his voice, but he knows my name. I cannot tell if he is really being nice to me or if he is playing a game that I do not know how to play. Maybe he did not see what a mess all the rings made on the table. I do not think he has noticed that I wet myself even though there is a small puddle on the floor. I really wish Mikey and Nicki were here in case I need them to play the three monkeys with. Then the man asks me a very strange question, "Ryan, how old are you right now?" Why does he care how old I am? That never stopped my mom or my dad from punishing me any way they felt like.

The man still has his hand on my shoulder, but instead of making me more nervous, it seems to be helping calm me down. Maybe not all grown-ups are the same. "I am nine years old right now," I say, hoping he cannot hear the fear in my voice. He grabs onto the back of the chair with both hands and slowly pulls it out of the corner with me still sitting on it. Please, God, not again. He then walks around the chair and drops down on one knee so he is pretty much face-to-face with me. He has such a kind face, and I think I just saw a tear run down his cheek. Why is he crying? I am the one who always does the crying. He tries his hardest to put a smile on his face, and then he sticks his hand out to me. I am very hesitant, but I reach out my hand to his, and he shakes my hand very gently, as if he is afraid he will hurt me if he shakes it too hard. Then he says, "My name is Dr. Frank, and I am here to help you, Ryan." Help me? What does he mean help me? Where was he while my dad was hurting me all the time? That is when I needed help. Why in the world am I wearing a hospital gown?

He is still looking right at me, but I am afraid to look at him, so I keep looking at the puddle on the floor. Looking at the puddle is making me think about all the water rings on the table, and I instantly start sweating and shaking again. I close my eyes and squeeze them shut as tight as I can. Even with my eyes closed, I can feel him staring at me. What does he want from me if it is not that? Then he stands back up, and as he starts walking back to the table he says, "Ryan, would you like to come join me back at the table?" Is he serious, join him back at the table? The table is where the water rings are. I do not want to be anywhere near that table. I know all too well what the punishment is for leaving water rings. No, thank you, Dr. Frank.

I watch him as he sits back down at the table. I am not positive, but I think he is looking right at the water rings. He stands back up and walks around to the other side of the table. He reaches into his pocket and takes out his handkerchief. It looks as if it has never been used. As he unfolds it, I can see the deep creases from being folded the same way for a long time. He shakes it out to loosen it up a bit and then he uses it to wipe up the water rings. I stand up and walk over to the table. I can't believe my eyes. The rings are completely gone. There is no trace of them at all. If only that magic had worked on our dining room table.

Dr. Frank walks back to the other side of the table and sits down in his chair. I want so much to ask him if I could use his handkerchief to wipe up the puddle I made on the floor, but I do not want to draw his attention to it in case he has not noticed it. I am too old to be wetting myself. I work up the courage to drag my chair back to the table and sit down across from him. I look up at him, and I can see that his eyes are still bloodshot, but he has stopped crying, which makes me feel better. I can tell he wants to ask me something, but he seems scared. I hate being scared; I don't want him to be scared either. "I am feeling better now, Dr. Frank. Is there something you would like to ask me?" I know we just met, but for some reason, I feel like I can trust him, like I already know him. In a very low, almost sympathetic voice he says, "Ryan, I am wondering if you could help me understand what was happening in your house the night both of your parents died?" Now I really wish Mikey and Nicki were here. I don't want to even think about my mom and dad, never mind what they did to me or especially how they died. There are still parts of it that I do not know and may never know.

"For some reason, Dr. Frank, I have been having some memory losses lately. It is almost like I fall asleep while I am still awake, if that makes any sense. I know it sounds weird, but it is the only way I can explain it. Sometimes it only lasts minutes, but sometimes it lasts hours or even days. I will tell you what I remember about how my parents died the best I can." I cannot understand why he is asking me about that night. Doesn't he know how horrible it was? All that blood…there was so much blood. I don't think he is trying to be mean. Maybe he is just nosy.

I am not sure where I should start. The less I have to actually think about it and talk about it, the better, so just a quick recap and then the last things I remember before the police took me away. "I can remember that my mom went from loving me way too much to hating me just enough. She knew what my dad was like when he drank too much, which happened more and more during those last six months. Sometimes life is funny, Dr. Frank. I think there is a word for what I mean by that. I think the word is 'karma.' You see, I have so many memories of hiding in my closet or under my bed whenever my dad would come home really late, because that meant he had been out drinking again. On those nights, I would hear my mom screaming for what seemed like hours because my dad was hurting her really bad. I never did anything to try to help my mom. I just hid until she stopped screaming and my dad started snoring on the couch. I think that is why when my dad started hurting me the same way, my mom never came to help me either.

"During those last few months, my mom had started taking some kind of medication that would knock her out almost instantly, and she would not get up for at least eight hours, if not more. It was her way of coping, I guess. I cannot even say for sure that my mom knew what my dad was actually doing to me. She may have thought that he was only beating me, as if that would not have been bad enough. Most of the times he abused me, my mom had been out of it for hours by the time he even came home. She may have never even heard my screams, but when I told her about my dad making me give him oral sex, she called me a liar and washed my mouth out with soap. I never told her that he had progressed to anally raping me. I believe in my heart that she knew everything he ever did to me. Like they say, 'Mothers always know.' I found it impossible to believe that her husband was raping her son under their own roof and she had no idea it was happening." I have to say Dr. Frank does not seem shocked by what I am telling him which is surprising to me. How many times have you heard about a father raping his own son? He is just sitting there looking at me and absorbing it all in. I hope I am not giving him any ideas. Please, God, not again.

"Dr. Frank, for you to better understand, I think I need to tell you about what happened the night before. On the nights that my dad would abuse me, my friends Mikey and Nicki would show up, and we would play the three-monkey game. It was the only way I could make it through what he would do to me. Every time we played, Mikey would be the hear-no-evil monkey, Nicki would be the see-no-evil monkey, and I would be the speak-no-evil monkey thanks to the fear my mom instilled in me when I confided in her about my dad. Nicki hated being the see-no-evil monkey all the time, so on that night, for the first time ever, I switched with her. I was the see-no-evil monkey, and she was the speak-no-evil monkey, which meant that Nicki saw what was happening with my dad for the very first time. And she was pissed! Once she heard my dad start snoring, she snuck into my mom's bedroom, found her pill bottle, and took two of the pills. I am not sure what she did with them. I was too afraid of her to ask." I cannot believe I am telling Dr. Frank all of this. I have never talked about Mikey and Nicki to anyone before. I sure hope I do not regret this. They are going to be so upset with me for talking about them while they are not here.

"This is where my memory jumps around more, Dr. Frank. I do remember that the next night my mom and dad got into a huge fight. I am not sure what it was about because I went and hid in my closet so I could not really hear what they were yelling at each other. I know my dad promised my mom he would not go out drinking again that night, which meant they would both be home with me all night. That thought frightened me more than hearing my dad unzipper his pants. I remember my mom started making dinner for us, I could smell spaghetti sauce simmering on the stove. My mom never really cooked for us, so this was something I was not used to. I thought maybe there was hope for as a family after all."

"That hope was very short-lived, Dr. Frank. You see, I did not realize that Nicki had other plans for that night. The anger from what she saw the night before was eating her alive. Mikey and I had promised to never tell her what was really happening when she heard the things she heard. We wanted to protect her as much as we could from the truth. It turned out that Nicki would be the one protecting us." I know he is not going to believe me, but I swear the next thing I knew, I was sitting at the dining room table with a knife in my hand. My mom was dead at one end of the table, and my dad was dead at the other end of the table. They were both covered in blood. There was blood everywhere.

53

DR. FRANK

I am sitting across from a twenty-eight-year-old man who, at this present moment, believes he is a nine-year-old boy. Tell me I do not have the best job in the world. I am going to help him if it is the last thing I do. It always amazes me when I deal with patients with dissociative identity disorder, how each individual personality has a different voice. When I was wondering if he had any other personalities besides Michael and Nicole, I did not even consider that he would have two different versions of himself, but he certainly does. The one sitting across from me now has the voice of a boy who has not gone through puberty yet. Fascinating.

I have been so caught up in everything that is happening that I did not notice we only had five minutes left of our session. I do not want to leave here today without knowing the rest of this story. I wonder, "Ryan, would it be okay with you if I called your doctor and asked if we could extend our session today?" Extending a session is frowned upon, but I really feel like today is the day that it all comes out. Luckily, he looks up at me and says, "I am okay with that, Dr. Frank, as long as I will not get punished." I take out my phone and call his doctor here at the facility, and he gives us permission to extend our session for thirty minutes. That should give me enough time, as long as I can get Michael and Nicole to come back out for me. I do not think there is anything else I can get from Ryan. He seems pretty certain that he does not know any more details of that night, and I believe he is being as truthful as he can be under the circumstances.

Considering our time is limited and I am not sure how to get Michael or Nicole back out, it might be time to confront Ryan about them. I was hoping to talk about this with his adult version, but he is not here either. How do I tell a nine-year-old boy that his best friends are not real? Here goes nothing. "Ryan, could I ask you about your friends Mikey and Nicki? I know you played hide-and-seek and the three monkeys with them, but did you ever do anything else with them? Did you ever go to the park with them or go riding bikes?"

Again, patients with this disorder differ in many ways. Some of them have no idea they have different personalities, while others know them all by name. Some of them can see the different personalities while others can only hear those personalities talking to them. I am having a hard time figuring out where Ryan fits in with all of that. I know he told me that Mikey and Nicki were both there with him the night his parents died, but he did not say if it was at the same time or at different times. I also remember he told me that he has not been able to see Michael and Nicole at the same time. Very interesting.

54

NICKI

Can someone please tell me what the hell is going on? The clock on the wall is telling me that it is only 10:00 a.m., so why am I not still in bed? It would also be really nice if someone could tell me who the hell this man is that is just staring at me like I am some kind of freak. I then realize that I am wearing a hospital gown, which has the distinct scent of urine coming from it. Am I in a hospital? Did something happen to me? If this man would actually say something instead of just staring at me, that would be helpful.

The man is starting to creep me out. That's it, I am out of here. I push my chair back and stand up. As I start heading toward the door, I can hear him say, "Where are you going, Ryan?" I stop midstep and freeze. Why in the world did he just call me Ryan? I turn around to face him without moving even an inch closer, and I ask him, "What did you just call me?" I wish I had a camera so I could show him the look he has on his face right now. It makes me think of the look someone would have if they had just seen a ghost, which we all know do exist.

"I am so sorry about that, Nicki. I got you mixed up with someone else. We still have about twenty-five minutes left.

Would you like to come sit back down?" Twenty-five minutes left for what? Who is this man, and what does he want from me? I am not comfortable with this, but what am I supposed to do? Make a run for it? How far would I get before he caught me, and then what? I slowly make my way back to the empty chair and sit down. He just sits there and smiles at me, again not saying a word. "You know my name is Nicki, so what is yours?" Help me out here, creepy man.

What he says next brings back so many bad memories all at once. I should have made a run for it when I had the chance. "My name is Frank, but you can call me Dr. Frank, if you like. I know a lot more about you than just your name. I know you have a twin brother named Mikey. I know you have a friend named Ryan that you and Mikey play games with all the time. I know the three of you created your own little private world that no one else was allowed into. I also know that you and Mikey were with Ryan in his house the night both of his parents died."

I look from him to the door. There is only about ten feet separating me from that damn door handle. The problem is that I would have to run right past him to get to it. What if I am not quick enough, and he grabs onto me before I make it to the door? I knew this day would come sooner or later. I told Mikey so many times that we could not trust Ryan to keep quiet. Then it hits me, Why am I here alone? Where is Mikey? Why is he not here with me? How much more does this man know? I guess there is only one way to find out. "It seems you know a lot about me, Frank. I am assuming you heard it all from Ryan, the little wimp. I knew it was a mistake letting him into our private world. All he ever did was complain about how his parents punished him, especially his dad. He made us play this stupid game with him he called three monkeys. I hated playing it, but I did it to shut him up. Him and Mikey always got to be the monkeys they wanted to be, and I was always stuck with the damn see-no-evil monkey. Who in their right mind wants to be a monkey that cannot see?" Hold up, Nicki, what are you doing? Why are you telling him things he may not already know? I am falling right into his little trap, stupid girl.

Let's see what else he already knows. "So, Frank, you said Ryan mentioned that Mikey and I were there with him when his parents died. What else did he tell you about that night?" Did Ryan really tell him everything that happened? Would he do that to me and Mikey after everything we did to help him? Damn it! I knew we couldn't trust him. Where the hell is Mikey? Frank seems unsure as to how to answer me. He is probably trying to come up with some big fat lie to trick me into telling him everything. I know how adults work. Lie to get whatever you want. Come on, Frank, spill it.

"To be completely honest with you, Ryan seems to have some memory issues around the time he was friends with you and Mikey. He told me everything he could remember, but there are bits and pieces missing that I was hoping Mikey or you could help fill in. Ryan told me that on the night before his parents died, you had snuck into his mom's bedroom and took two of the pills she used to sleep, but he does not know what you did with them. He also told me that the next day, his parents got into a huge fight about something. This resulted in his dad promising to not go out that night to get drunk, which scared him a lot. He then remembers smelling spaghetti sauce simmering on the stove as his mom was making dinner for them. The next thing he remembers is sitting at the dining room table with a knife in his hands and being covered with his parents' blood. His mom was dead at one end of the table, and his dad was dead at the other end. Then the cops came and took him away."

Well, Ryan, it seems I was right about you all along. I knew you would be the one to tattle on us. You had Mikey fooled, but

I was always the smarter one, the braver one, the protector. The only girl in a group of three, and I had to be the one to take care of us all. After everything I did for you, this is how you pay me back. I hope you are finally proud of yourself, you little wimp. If you had only stood up to me that night and not switched monkeys with me, we would not be in all this trouble. Where the hell is Mikey? He is not innocent in all of this either.

"Sounds like Ryan squealed like a pig to you, Frank. He always was the weak one out of the three of us. I guess it is time to confess my sins, though I am not so sure they were sins. Between the three of us, we could not figure out another way to stop what was happening, and trust me Frank, it needed to be stopped. The night before it all happened, I was finally allowed to be the speak-no-evil monkey instead of the see-no-evil one. Mikey and Ryan had been lying to me about what was really happening during the times I could not see. So that night, when I saw what was actually happening to make Ryan cry like that, I was horrified.

"I may not have liked Ryan very much and definitely did not trust him, but he was still a friend of mine and my brother's best friend. If they were not strong enough to do something about it, then that meant I had to. Yes, I snuck into his mom's bedroom, and yes, I took two of her sleeping pills.

"When we found out both of his parents were going to be home that next night, I came up with a plan. I thought through every detail to make sure my plan was flawless. The waiting was killing me. The idea of chickening out was not an option. Once his dad came home from work, my excitement grew. The time was near. Then just like clockwork, his dad was on the couch watching television, ignoring us as usual when he was sober. His mom was in the kitchen making dinner. She asked Ryan to set the table for them like I knew she would, and the plan went into action. I put out plates for the three of us along with the silverware. I then filled three glasses with iced cold water, which was pretty much all there ever was in the house to drink that was not liquor. I took one of the pills out of my pocket and crushed it up as small as I could with the back of the fork at his mom's seat and dropped it into her glass. It was crushed up so small that it just looked like tiny pieces from the ice. I wiped off the fork with the bottom of my T-shirt to make sure she could not taste anything that might be left between the tines. I then did the same thing to his dad's glass of water."

Am I really going to do this? Am I going to tell this man who calls himself Dr. Frank all the details of that night? Is there any point in not finishing after everything I just told him and what Ryan already told him? I feel like I am betraying Mikey, but he is the one who is not here helping me deal with this. Where the hell are you, Mikey? I hope he forgives me for what I am about to do. "Those pills worked like magic, Frank. The three of us sat down at the table, the same table with those damn water rings all over it, and we ate our last meal together as a so-called family. I sat there eating my spaghetti and meatballs, but my attention was on those two glasses of water. I watched as they both drank it down, one big gulp at a time. What good is ice water if you wait for the ice to melt before you drink it? I even got up and refilled their glasses for them, not that either of them thanked me for it. About halfway through their plates of spaghetti, they both started yawning, and I couldn't help but smile on the inside. The plan was going just as I hoped."

Once again, I wish I had a camera with me so I could take a picture of Frank's face. He looks absolutely horrified, as if he can already guess what is coming next. He is sitting on the edge of his chair, and I don't think he has blinked in the last ten minutes. He is hanging on my every word. Can't stop now. That just would not be right. "His dad was the first one to drift off to la-la land. Just as I was about to bite into my last meatball, I heard his head smash right into his plate of spaghetti. He was out for the count. His mom just sat there and laughed. She had no idea what was happening. I got up to get myself another meatball and some more sauce. His mom didn't cook often, but when she did, it was always delicious. *Why not enjoy it while you can?* was my thought. I think it took his mom longer to pass out because she had been using the pills for some time, but the next thing I knew, it was her turn. Face-down in her plate, just like his dad. It wasn't that I hated his mom like I hated his dad after seeing what he was doing to Ryan, but I needed her to be out of it too so I could do what needed to be done without her trying to stop me. I knew they would be out for hours, so I took my time finishing my dinner and my nice glass of ice-cold water."

I have to admit, it feels good to finally talk about this. It is not easy to live through something like we did and not have anyone to talk about it with. Frank is either a good listener, or he is so terrified of what I am saying that he has lost his ability to speak. "Once I was full, I washed my plate and silverware in the sink like his mom always made us do, and then it was time for the next part of the plan. Frank, are you sure you want me to tell you what happened next? It gets kind of messy." Better to be safe than sorry. He has the best facial expressions I have ever seen. He might actually be in a state of shock. He shakes his head just a little bit and says, "Please continue, Nicki. You are doing great so far."

You asked for it, Frank. "Once I was done cleaning up after myself, I went and grabbed the rope that Ryan's mom would use to tie him to the chair whenever she put him in the corner, I also grabbed the sharpest knife I could find. I cut the rope into six pieces, three for his mom and three for his dad. I started with his mom. I used one piece of rope to tie her hands behind her back, and the other two I used to tie both of her legs to the legs of the chair. Her face was a mess. It was all covered with spaghetti sauce, and she even had some spaghetti stuck in her hair. Then I moved on to his dad, the evilest man I have ever met. I tied him up the same way I had tied up his mom. Truth be told, I may have pulled those ropes tighter than I needed to, but he did not even move a muscle. Those were some good pills, Frank. Once I had them both tied up, it was time for my final part of the plan. You may want to block your ears for this part. As I stood there just looking at his dad tied to that chair, spaghetti sauce all over his ugly face, the only thing I kept seeing was what I saw him doing to Ryan the night before, and then I started remembering all the times I heard Ryan screaming and crying for him to stop. His own damn dad doing that to him… I knew I had to stop it from happening again, so I did. I grabbed onto his chair and pulled it away from the table, so he was facing me. I undid his belt, and then I unzipped his pants. It was not as easy as I thought it would be with him tied to the chair, but I managed to work his pants down to his knees. I opened the fly on his boxer shorts and grabbed onto his penis with one hand, then with the other hand I sliced it right off. That woke him up. Good thing I had tied him extra tight. He couldn't move. He started bleeding all over the place. Then he started to scream, so I did the only thing I could do. I shoved his penis into his own mouth just like he did to Ryan all those times. I sat back down in my chair and just watched him while he continued to bleed and choke to death. Luckily, Ryan's mom was out cold and didn't even move a muscle. She did let out a quiet little snore every once in a while, which was sort of soothing. Once I knew he was dead, I took his penis out of his mouth and chopped it up into tiny little pieces then flushed it down the toilet. Good riddance.

"Once I was done with my plan, and I knew we were finally safe, I left, and I never went back. I never saw Ryan or Mikey again. It was best that we kept our distance, that we had no contact with each other at all. It was not an easy decision to make considering Mikey and I are twins and had spent every day of our lives together, but I did what needed to be done at whatever the cost."

I cannot believe I just told this stranger called Frank everything that happened that night, everything that I made happen that night, but I do have to admit it feels really good to tell the truth after all this time.

55

DR. FRANK

There are not even words to explain how I am feeling right now. I have so many different thoughts and emotions interacting that I cannot even think straight. I guess I should have at least suspected that if he has two different versions of himself, it would only make sense that he would also have the same for his "friends." The second I heard that squeaky little girlish voice, I knew I was meeting Nicki. I will admit I was not ready for her. I thought Ryan was still with me. To hear her confess to her part in what happened that night chilled me to the bone. She talked about it like she was talking about taking a dog for a walk. When she said she sat back down and just watched Ryan's dad bleed and choke on his own penis until he was dead, I felt like I was watching an episode of Dateline.

There are a few things that are really bothering me at this point. The first being, now that I know for sure how his dad died, there is no way he will ever be released from this facility, and even after hearing everything I have so far, that bothers me. The second thing being, if what Nicki just told me was the truth, then who killed Ryan's mom? The third thing being, who called the cops? I am so much closer to knowing what really happened in that house before the murders and even more importantly, how the murders themselves happened. I am guessing in the next twelve minutes I need to meet Mikey to fill in the last missing pieces.

My throat is so dry from just sitting here with my mouth hung wide open, as if I were trying to catch flies, the entire time Nicki was telling me about her part of what happened. Luckily, there is some water left in the pitcher, though I am sure by now it is room temperature. I finish what was left in my glass and then refill it. There is only about a half of a glass left in the pitcher, and I can see that Nicki's glass is almost empty, so I offer to fill it for her. "Nicki, would you like me to fill your glass for you? It is not very cold, but it is yours if you want it."

"Dude, do I look like my sister to you?" Well, hello there, Mikey, and just in time. I knew this was going to be a session I would never forget. In one session I have been able to speak to Bryant, Ryan, Nicole, Nicki, Michael, and now Mikey. I am so glad I decided to turn my recorder app on when Nicki showed up.

CHAPTER

56

MIKEY

Have you ever felt like you just stepped into the twilight zone? Where am I? Why am I dressed in a hospital gown? Who is this man offering me water, and why did he just call me Nicki? I know we are twins and look a lot alike but come on. The man is just sitting there looking at me with a big grin on his face, and then he says, "Would you like the rest of the water, Mikey?" Interesting, this strange man not only knows Nicki's name, but he also knows my name. I am kind of thirsty. "Yeah, sure, fill it up. Sorry, I didn't catch your name." Might as well get on his good side just in case I am in trouble for something again. "My name is Frank, but you can call me Dr. Frank if you like." Why would I want to call him Dr. Frank? He is not dressed like any doctor I have ever seen. He pours the rest of the water into my glass, sits back down, and just stares at me.

As I go to grab my glass, he breaks the silence. "So, Mikey, I had a long talk with your sister Nicki this morning. She was telling me about the night your friend Ryan's parents died. Unfortunately, she left before I had a chance to ask her a couple more questions. Do you think you might be able to answer them for me?" What did he just say? Nicki was telling him about what? Why would she do that without talking to me about it first? Is this really happening, or am I in the midst of a very bad dream I cannot wake up from? Nicki always said the day would come when we would have to face the music. Seems she was right, just like every other time.

Let's get it over with. "I guess that depends on what your questions are, but I can give it a try." If I knew this was how the day was going to go, I would have stayed away.

"We don't have much time left today, but if you could answer two questions for me, I think we will be all set. While I was talking to Nicki, she confessed to what she did to Ryan's dad, but according to her story, when she left, his mom was still alive. She was tied to the chair and out cold from the sleeping pill, but still alive. So if it was not Nicki that killed her, who did?"

This is really happening after all this time.

Time to sing like a canary. "I can help you with that one, Frank. You have to understand, Ryan was my best friend. I mean, yes, he could be a pain in the butt at times. Sorry, bad choice of words there. He could get on my nerves at times and always wanted to play the same games, but we did have some great times together. When he confided in me about how his mom would tie him to a chair and put him in a corner for hours at a time or lock him in the closet if he so much as looked at her the wrong way, I couldn't believe it. As we became closer friends, he confided in me even more. He told me about how his mom had made him breastfeed all those years until his dad walked in on them. Man, that was messed up. Then he told me about how his mom made him sit under scalding-hot water in the shower and washed his mouth out with soap when he was finally brave enough to tell her about what his dad was doing to him. It was my idea for him to tell her. He didn't think it was a good idea, but I talked him into doing it."

221

All these years later, and yet as I sit here telling this strange man named Frank about what happened, I can still see it clear as day. I feel like I am reliving it all over again. "That night when I showed up, Nicki had already left. Ryan's dad was sitting there tied to his usual seat, his pants were pulled down to his knees, and there was blood all over his crotch area. I was too afraid to look any closer. It was obvious that he was dead. Ryan's mom was tied to her seat as well, and although she looked a mess with spaghetti sauce all over her face, she was sleeping, not dead. I just stood there looking at the mess Nicki had left behind. I knew it was her who had killed his dad. She was so horrified and disgusted by what she had seen the night before, there was no way she was going to let it go unpunished."

My throat is so dry from all this talking. I reach over and grab my glass of water, drink the rest of it down in one big gulp, and then finish the story. "I completely understood why Nicki did what she did. She knew Ryan was too weak to ever do anything about it, and it was obvious his bitch of a mother was never going to help him either. Then I started hearing his mom making some kind of noise. It wasn't a snore. It was more like she was groaning or moaning in her sleep. I started freaking out. What if she was waking up and saw me there with her husband dead across from her, and she was tied to her seat? I panicked! I picked up the knife Nicki had used on Ryan's dad and went over to his mom. As I stood there looking down on her, I kept hearing all the horrible things that she had done to Ryan all those years over and over in my head, and I just lost it. I followed Nicki's example. She took the knife to his dad's crotch because that is how he hurt Ryan, so I took the knife and I sliced off his mom's boobs one at a time. She woke up after I sliced the first one off, but by the time she had a chance to start screaming, I had already sliced off the second one. Blood…so much blood all over the place. I ran as fast as I could to the kitchen sink and threw up what looked like spaghetti and meatballs. His mom was still screaming so I grabbed the dish towel and shoved it in her mouth to keep her quiet. After a couple of minutes, she stopped moving, and then she stopped breathing. Once I knew she was dead, I got out of there as quick as I could."

I have never told that story to anyone before. I still cannot believe that I did what I did to Ryan's mom. I just kept thinking about everything she had already done to him in the past, never mind what would happen if she woke up and he was sitting there with his dad the way he was. She probably would have killed Ryan, and I couldn't let that happen.

"I think that answers your question, Frank. What was your second one?" No matter what his second question is, it can't be worse than his first one. "Thank you for being so open and honest with me, Mikey, I truly appreciate it. My other question I had for you is, Do you know who called the police?" Now that is something I have never even thought about. "To be honest with you, Frank, I have no idea who called the cops. I got out of there as quick as I could. If I had stayed any longer, I would have ended up throwing up again. There was so much blood all over the place. If I had to guess who called them, it would have had to be either a neighbor who had heard his mom screaming before I could get the dish towel in her mouth or Ryan himself. I did see Ryan a few times after that night. I even went to his parents' funerals with him. I think that was the last time we saw each other."

Frank looks disappointed. I told him everything I remember even though I really did not want to. "Sorry I can't answer that one for you, Frank, but if Ryan says it was not him, then it had to have been a neighbor. It sure as hell was not Nicki or me, and there was no one else there who could have made the call except Ryan." He looks at me with a sad look on his face, and he says, "Do you think Ryan would speak to me again?" How would I know the answer to that? I have no idea where Ryan is. I hope he doesn't think I am rude, but I really need to take a leak, so I gotta split.

CHAPTER

57

RYAN

"Dr. Frank, I think our time is up. It is just about 10:30 a.m., according to the clock over there. Do you think they forgot to come get me? I don't want either of us to get in any trouble." I do have to say that was a very fast half hour. It seems like he just called my other doctor to get permission to extend our session, and now it is over. I wonder if he has any aspirin. My head is really splitting right now. I hate when I get headaches like this. It hasn't happened in a while, but when it does, it really stinks.

He grabs onto his cell phone and brings it to life. I wish I was allowed to have a cell phone. "According to my phone, we have two minutes left Ryan, which is just enough time for my last question. After speaking with both Nicki and Mikey, it is still unclear who called the police the night your parents died. Do you happen to know who made that call?" Are we still talking about that? I thought we were done. This Frank guy really asks a lot of questions, but he did say it was his last one, so…"As a matter of fact, Frank, I do know who made the call to the cops that night. It was me. Remember I told you I was having a lot of memory losses back then? Well, like I told you already, I can remember smelling the spaghetti sauce simmering in the kitchen and then the next thing I remember, I was sitting at the dining room table with the knife in my hands. I was nine years old, and my mom and dad were both dead. I didn't know what else to do, so I called the cops and told them my mom and dad were dead. I knew I had not killed them, so I had nothing to worry about.

"There is one other thing I do remember about that night, Frank. After I called the cops, I went and sat back in my seat at the table. There was blood all over the place. I don't know why I did it, but I picked up my water glass, and I started making rings in the blood all over the table while I waited for the cops to show up. Once I heard all the sirens getting closer, I put the water glass down and picked up the knife. I was going to go wash it in the sink like my mom would have wanted me to, but one of the cops busted down the door and took it from me. They started asking me all kinds of questions, but I did not answer any of them. I guess a part of me knew that Nicki and Mikey must have killed my mom and dad, and I did not want to get them in trouble, so I never said a word about anything that had happened in our house until now."

CHAPTER
58

DR. FRANK

The next thing I know the orderly is opening the door to escort Ryan back to his room. That was one of, if not the most exciting sessions I have ever had in my career. I doubt very much I will ever have another one that will ever compare. I now know the whole true story of what happened in that house. Starting with the years of abuse he suffered at the hands of both his mom and his dad and ending with how they both died, as well as by whom. There were so many pieces to the puzzle, but one by one, they all fell into place.

I am still having a very hard time wrapping my head around how parents could do such things to a child that they brought into this world. Although I do not believe murder is ever the right answer, I can say that I completely understand how it was the only answer to a nine-year-old boy living in those circumstances. What other option did he have? Now I have to decide what to do with all this information. The right thing to do would be to give the recording to the police and let them do with it what they like. Ryan was already convicted of the murders and will never be released, so I am not sure what good it would do to turn the recording over to them. Even though he believes in his mind he did not kill them, the truth is he did; he just doesn't know it. Maybe it is better to leave it that way. Hasn't he already been through enough? I think it will be best for me to take a couple of days off before deciding my course of action. I do not want to be responsible for causing him any more pain.

As I pack up my stuff to leave, I can't help but think back to when I first found out I was going to be allowed to work with the boy. I was not sure I would be able to get through to him after so many other therapists had failed, but I sure was hopeful. Then I remember the first time we actually met face-to-face in my office and he looked out my window, and when I asked him what he saw, instead of saying "The sky" or "Clouds" or "Buildings," he said "Freedom." I will never forget that moment. I felt an instant connection with him. I am glad he learned to trust me enough to bring me into his private world, even though it was as an Uber driver.

I will spend the rest of the day writing up my report on the boy, as most of the world knows him, and then work on figuring out the best thing I can do with what I now know. God, I hope I make the right decision.

EPILOGUE

To whom it may concern:

If you are reading this it means I have finally found the freedom I have been waiting so long for. I have been locked away in this place for two-thirds of my life, not that it was much of a life. For the last nineteen years, I have been haunted by the deaths of my parents. I never told anyone about our family's dirty little secrets. My mother always told me I should speak no evil, and I never wanted to cross that woman.

I want it to be known that for all the years I have been locked away in here, I had always believed that I was innocent of killing my mother and father, even though the courts found me guilty. I never said a word to anyone because I believed I was protecting the two people who protected me when I needed it the most. I guess we can all make ourselves believe anything we really want to.

As the twentieth anniversary of their deaths approached, I decided it was time that I finally tried to remember what had happened in our house that night. I knew there were parts that I had locked away in the back of my mind. I just had to find a way to bring them back out. The only hope I had of making that happen was to stop taking my medications, so that is what I did. I started spitting them into the toilet instead of swallowing them. After about a month, they seemed to be out of my system. During that month, I started spending more and more time in my own little private world. I avoided making contact with anyone so they would not notice my mood changes.

Once I made it to about five weeks, I started getting some of my older memories back. I started remembering some of things that my parents did to me when I was a little boy. As more and more time went by, I started having very vivid flashbacks. The strange thing about these flashbacks is that sometimes when I saw myself, I was someone else. Sometimes I was another boy about my age whose name was Mikey. There were even times when I was Mikey's twin sister, Nicki. Can you imagine seeing yourself as a girl? It took me some time to understand what it was I was actually seeing, but once I did and I accepted it as my true reality, everything became so much clearer.

This morning, the flashbacks kept happening over and over again. I was getting closer to knowing the truth about my parents' deaths, but the closer I got, the more scared I became. Time to be a man, I had to know for sure one way or the other. I went into my bathroom and turned on the shower as hot as it would go. I closed the door and waited for the bathroom to fill with steam. I took off my hospital gown and climbed in the shower. I sat down on the floor of the shower like an Indian and just let the scalding-hot water rain down on me. I welcomed all the memories, all the flashbacks to come to the surface.

I started reliving my last day in our house, our last day as a family. I could hear my parents arguing. I could smell the spaghetti sauce simmering. Then I could see myself as Nicki setting the table for my mother. Then she was crushing up the pills she took from my mother's room the night before, and she was putting one in each of my parents' glasses of ice water. Then I could see my father's face smashing into his plate of spaghetti, and then my mother doing the same thing. When the next flashback played out, I knew what I had done. Nicki was the tough one of us, that was for sure. She found the rope my mother had tied me to the chair with and used it to tie my mother and my father to their chairs. I thought I was going to be sick when I saw what she did next. She pulled my father's pants down and cut his penis off. She then shoved it in his own mouth to stop him from screaming. I am not sure if he bled to death or choked to death. Her final act that night was chopping his penis into tiny little pieces and flushing it down the toilet.

In the next set of flashbacks, I saw myself as Mikey finding my father the way Nicki left him and my mother starting to make noises at the other end of the table. Then he grabbed the same knife Nicki used on my father, and he cut both of my mother's breasts right off. Blood went squirting all over the place, and my mother started screaming, so Mikey grabbed the dish towel and shoved it in her mouth to keep her quiet.

After spending the last almost twenty years of my life believing I was an innocent man, I realized I was guilty the whole time. How can I live with myself, knowing that I killed my own mother and father? They were monsters that destroyed my life, but doesn't that make me a monster too by taking their lives? I got out of the shower, dried off, grabbed a notepad and a pen, and wrote this, my confession for my sins and my suicide note. Once I am done writing this, I am going to get the razor blade that I have had hidden in my mattress for years, climb back into the shower, and kill the only monster left of the Hughes family. Sorry about the mess.

Sincerely,
Ryan Frank Hughes
The Boy

ACKNOWLEDGMENTS

I have been an avid reader for about fifteen years now. I typically read murder mysteries or suspenseful dramas. I had the storyline for this book floating around in my head for about five years. At times I could see it playing out in my mind as if I were at a movie theater. I kept waiting for someone to write a book dealing with the many different, somewhat dark subject matters, but I never found one.

I would first like to thank *Nicole*, for her constant support and for believing in me more than I believed in myself. If it was not for you telling me I could do this, you would not be reading this right now.

Next, I would like to thank *Steve*, the absolute best friend anyone could ever ask for. You have always been there for me no matter what. I am so grateful for your friendship. It means the world to me.

Lastly, thank you to you, the reader who took a chance on a brand-new author. I hope you enjoyed reading *The Boy* as much as I enjoyed writing it for you.

ABOUT THE AUTHOR

Alan Sakell was born and raised in Fall River, Massachusetts, which is best known as the city where Lizzie Borden took an axe. He works in accounting for a nonprofit organization in the city of Boston and now resides just north of Boston.

CPSIA information can be obtained
at www.ICGtesting.com
Printed in the USA
LVHW090545230222
711617LV00005BA/147